PENGUIN BOOKS

SUNDAY AFTERNOONS

Julie Mitchell was born in Cheshire but moved with her
family to Northern Ireland when she was seven. She was
educated at the Methodist College, Belfast, then returned
to England to study modern languages at Bristol University.
She spent some time travelling in Italy and Germany and
now lives in a farmhouse on the edge of Bodmin Moor with
her husband and two children.

GW00726106

Sunday Afternoons

Julie Mitchell

PENGUIN BOOKS

PENGUIN BOOKS

Published by the Penguin Group
27 Wrights Lane, London W8 5TZ, England
Viking Penguin Inc., 40 West 23rd Street, New York, New York 10010, USA
Penguin Books Australia Ltd, Ringwood, Victoria, Australia
Penguin Books Canada Ltd, 2801 John Street, Markham, Ontario, Canada L3R 1B4
Penguin Books (NZ) Ltd, 182–190 Wairau Road, Auckland 10, New Zealand

Penguin Books Ltd, Registered Offices: Harmondsworth, Middlesex, England

First published by Viking 1988
Published in Penguin Books 1989
1 3 5 7 9 10 8 6 4 2

Copyright © Julie Mitchell, 1988
All rights reserved

Printed and bound in Great Britain by
Hazell Watson & Viney Limited
Member of BPCC Limited
Aylesbury, Bucks, England

1

On the first Friday evening in July they held the big dance in Ballynahinch. The Indians were to play there – all the girls went mad for them – and afterwards, Noreen knew that nothing would ever be the same again.

It all began one Sunday, those days when she used to walk the roads with Eileen McAllister, arm in arm, secure in companionship. What else was there to do, after all, on a Sunday? At fifteen they were past the age of running through boggy fields, or sitting in lazy living-rooms with parents.

During the week they would meet beneath the big clock of the Lisburn town hall, after Noreen had come up from the city on the bus. She went to the Methodist school in Belfast, where her Da had gone as a boy, and where the windows were criss-crossed with Sellotape. Sometimes there were bomb scares, which meant no classes, but they did make your heart beat, like when you were stopped in the roadblocks at night, and you wondered if it wasn't the soldiers at all but terrorists, who'd ask you which you were, and if you said the wrong thing then they'd blow your head off. People were known to get their cars hijacked, and there were parts of the city where you couldn't go, if you were on the wrong side.

After school, Noreen walked into the centre of the city,

past the big bright paintings of King Billy on his white horse and the walls scrawled with NO SURRENDER or NO POPE HERE. Sometimes it was BRITS OUT or UP THE PROVOS, and she walked quickly then.

She caught the bus at the station beside the bridge, where there were trains and newspaper stands and a smell of toilets. The bus came out of Belfast through the back streets, past wee junk shops and bars and waste land where the houses had been razed to the ground. Some houses and shops had the windows boarded up, but there were still people living in them, and once there were soldiers scuttling in the doorways with their rifles out. The woman sitting in front of Noreen put her bag up to the window, but it wouldn't have done her much good, and the bus just drove on, anyway.

It took half an hour to get up to Lisburn, and there Eileen would be waiting on her beneath the clock, clutching her satchel of books. They wandered around the shops together, looking in windows with steamy breath and planning what they would buy, if they ever had the money: shoes and skirts and jeans and tops and belts and dresses . . . Oh, they could buy clothes, all right.

They knew that one day there'd be work and a weekly wage, every young girl's dream, before she settles down and marries some local boy. Then they get some wee council house on the outskirts of town, if they're lucky. Otherwise they have to spend the first years with the parents, or in a mobile home on the family farm, if they're country people. They have babies and no money, but they make it to the pub every Friday, or at least the husband does. For the wife there's the kids to look after

6

and housework to be done; maybe a visit to her sister-in-law or her mother – highlight of the week.

You have to make the most of clothes and the like before that happens. A job, money – what wouldn't they do then! That freedom was what they lived for, though you couldn't expect it to last, of course. It was a sort of golden age, to which every teenager looked forward and every married person looked back. It was the time of freedom before marriage, and responsibility.

Meanwhile they made do with family cast-offs and the occasional birthday or Christmas treat; there was pocket money, but that was a joke, for all it would buy you. They girned about school uniform but were secretly glad of it, for no one knew if you had nice clothes or not. And you could wear the skirts short and tight, heels high and clumpy, and stockings too. But at Eileen's convent school the nuns were strict, and the girls had to wear knee-length socks and flat shoes. Eileen hated the nuns – mean ould bitches, she said. They wouldn't even let you away with a touch of make-up, and that was why, above all, she loved to go into Willis's, where they had everything – eyeshadow, lipstick, mascara, eyeliner – oh, everything!

They pretended they wanted to buy and tried the lot, giggling, while the girl behind the counter frowned. She wore two studs in her nose and thought herself very superior, because they were still at school and she was earning, boring though it was; and because of the studs, of course.

Occasionally, feeling bold, they would nick bits of make-up – just a small container of blue eyeshadow or ruby lipshine. Most often they took sweets, because that was easier, and wouldn't be so serious if you got caught.

If you did get nicked then the shop would inform your parents and even the school, and you'd be in disgrace, for everyone would know. It gave you a thrill, though, when you got away with it, and you forgot the fear of the plain-clothes detective which made you feel guilty at night.

Another place they went on those days was Mc-Cauley's, the cake shop in Bridge Street. They often had messages to do there – soda and wheaten to buy, or maybe some scones, and very occasionally a chocolate roll, if there were visitors expected at home. It was wonderful just standing by the glass, watching the girls at work. They filled white boxes with the fragile shells of chocolate-topped cream buns, deftly wrapped crusty white loaves, still warm from the oven, or shovelled up iced buns with almonds on. Upstairs you could sit down and get a frothy milk shake and a custard slice, or a cup of tea and a bit of golden fruit-cake. They never had any money left afterwards, but it didn't matter. There was always next week.

The boot boys used to congregate just over the road from McCauley's, where there was a wall low enough to sit on. They would be drinking Coca-Cola and eating hamburgers which they'd got from the corner café. They smoked and whistled as you went by, making you blush, or sometimes they cursed and made your ears burn. Not that you cared really, but still.

On Sundays, though, the shop eyes were closed, the streets strangely sleeping, and you wondered how they could ever have been busy with people. The place was

like a bombed town; there was only an occasional policeman snooping with a gun, or an armoured car bristling
with green soldiers.

What did they do at night? It must be romantic to love
one of them, for they would either be killed in a bomb,
or shot, perhaps – or else they'd go away home to
England and you'd never see them again. Either way,
you'd escape the mundaneness which kills passion.

Noreen's Ma sometimes invited Englishmen home
from the barracks where she worked, but they were
never the young ones, always the older ones from the
offices. Ma said she felt sorry for them, stuck here, where
they weren't liked. They were only trying to do a job,
after all. And so far from their families. Da wasn't keen
on it, for it disturbed his Sunday (which he offered up
to the Lord), but Ma said that this was her way of being
Christian.

The Englishmen spoke funny, and Noreen and Eileen
had to keep saying, 'What?'; then Noreen's Ma would
say, 'You mean "Pardon".' Home was heavy and stale
on those afternoons, though the mornings were all right
– late and bright, no school, and you could smell the
roast when you came in from church: just as Sundays
had always been.

Da was saved, and sang in the choir every Sunday. A
quite short, tidy man, who liked his trousers well
pressed and wore silver armbands to keep up his shirt
sleeves. He had grey-blue eyes, which sparkled as he
sang, and a lovely smile. His dark, almost black hair was
always combed and sleek with cream, and the top of his
head shone through the fine strands like a smooth egg.

Noreen and Ma used to watch him from their pew in

church, but he never looked their way because he was busy reading from his hymn-book along with all the other men and women. He wore a tie and stiff collar which pinched his neck, and his hair was clipped very short at the back. He helped to give out the hymn-books at the door as the people came in, and once he did the reading, looking very small, even schoolboyish – as if he were on his best behaviour – before the lectern where the great Bible rested open. He cleared his throat frequently, and when Noreen heard his familiar voice echoing in the vastness of the church, it seemed as if she were hearing him for the first time. That was a long time ago, when Da did the reading, long before Ma ever started inviting the men home from the barracks, or Noreen ran the roads with Eileen.

Things were different in those days, when Noreen was wee – but even then, Sundays were stagnant days; it seemed like she was washed up in a backwater where nothing much went on. They went to church twice, once in the morning, when Noreen had Sunday school too, then again in the evening, and Da went on to the Meeting afterwards.

On Sunday mornings then, while Da got dressed in the bathroom, Ma helped Noreen learn her verses for Sunday school, and she got the sandwiches and buns ready for the Meeting in the evening. Da would be hounding her for a clean shirt, which he couldn't see, even though it was right before his eyes in the linen cupboard, and Noreen's shoes were often discovered to be dirty at the last minute. Still, Ma always managed to be ready herself, all posh in her court shoes and good cream coat (or the heavy maroon one in winter), and her brown curly hair sitting lovely beneath her fawn hat. She would have her cream handbag, or else her maroon one, over her arm, and sometimes she wore thin lacy gloves as well. Noreen had some like that: white, flimsy things, which she hated and wore only on very special occasions, like for the Thanksgiving.

On fine days the three of them walked over to the church, but if it rained, or was very cold, or they were late, then Da drove them over in the red company car which he cleaned and polished every Saturday afternoon. At the end of a hymn you could sometimes hear the rain hammering, and then the church seemed like a great umbrella sheltering them all huddled together inside it, a veritable flock. But often when they surfaced, the sun was shining, and Noreen and Ma would stroll back home, leaving Da to follow later when all the books were tidied away and the chatting done. Noreen's step was light because church was over and the day fine and it was nearly lunchtime. Ma smiled and waved to people as the cars roared off, and Noreen could feel that she was happy too.

In autumn when the blackberries were ripe, they would stop to pick them in the hedgerows and stand there eating them. The juicy tartness burst over their tongues, stinging their gums, and Noreen had a delicious feeling of forbiddenness, or of truancy, somehow, standing there together with Ma, eating blackberries in the sunshine on a Sunday. Ma's face, which curved like an angel's, shone, and her lips glowed black with the fruit. Still, she always managed to have the potatoes on by the time Da walked in through the door and kissed her on the cheek.

After lunch, when there were no visitors, Da would prepare himself for the evening Meeting. He sat in the straightbacked armchair by the window with his Bible, ruler, pen and notebook, carefully looking things up and underlining important verses in red and making notes. He liked there to be quiet, or else he couldn't concentrate properly – and it was Sunday, after all. He wouldn't let Ma hang out the washing, and it was best if she could try to have most of the work for the dinner done the day before, for they must honour the Lord's Day. Not that Da was one for laying down the law; he just quietly insisted, as was his way.

They always said Grace before meals – at least, Da did, but when he wasn't there, then they didn't bother. Da liked to hear about what Noreen had learnt in Sunday school that day – the stories of Jesus healing and performing miracles with bread and fish – and once he told Noreen that she must ask the Lord Jesus into her heart (but Ma said later, don't you worry your head about it, Noreen!). Oh, Sundays were long.

Sundays were days of suits and hats and dresses, roasts and fullness and boredom – the quietness of the clock ticking. Ma put on her glasses with the tortoiseshell rims and read a book – a romance, or sometimes a thriller; or, when the dining-table was cleared after dinner, the mats put away, the crumbs brushed off and the linen tablecloth folded up, she would sit writing letters on its dark, polished surface, pen tapping her teeth while she thought, then a steady scratching on the pad of paper. She smiled to herself now and then. She wrote to the relatives in Annalong, and to Grandma on the farm, and to the sister who had moved away over the water when she married; she'd married some boy in the forces and now she lived in London, a place with a magical ring to it.

On Sunday afternoons Granny Logan sometimes came to tea with her bad leg and angina. She walked with a stick, which alarmed Noreen, and she watched with small, sharp eyes behind glasses. More often, though, they all went to the big house in Moira, and then Granda was there too with his feet up, watching the football on TV, unless Granny Logan told him not to.

Granny used to see to people's feet until she got her bad leg – you could see great blue veins bulging through her thick yellow stockings – and people still came to the house sometimes to have them done. It was a house of dark furniture, including a piano, and cut glass and floral sofas. Noreen had to be careful not to move too fast in it, or else she knocked over some precious ornament and there was a great fuss. Granny pursed her lips and tutted, and Ma tried to clear up the mess whilst apologizing, then Granda got up from the football and tried to help in his clumsy way. Finally Granny Logan shooed them all out of the way and cleared it up herself, grunting as she got down on her elderly knees and breathing hard, so they'd all know what a trial it was for her; but none of them could do it properly, she said, shaking her head wearily.

Presently she would wheel in the trolley with the strong orange tea steaming in fragile china cups and pink wafer biscuits sitting on a matching china plate which had a white paper doily on. Sometimes there were dainty sandwiches made with thin white bread and butter and some sort of meat paste. There was talk of Granny's health – what the Doctor said last week – and church, and Daddy's work, which Granda liked to hear about.

Noreen fidgeted and was allowed out into the garden, where the borders were neatly trimmed and the grass mown in regimented strips. She fitted her feet into the lines of the crazy paving, swung around the whirligig and ran her hand along the top of the wooden fence at the edge of the lawn.

Back inside, Ma would be clearing away the dishes for Granny Logan, and Granda in front of the TV again, his slippered feet comfortably resting on a wee polished table, one of a nest. He took them down guiltily when the door opened, but smiled when he saw that it was only Noreen and put them back with a sigh of satisfaction, or relief. Sometimes, when they were alone, he slipped her 10p, once even a 50p piece, with his finger to his lips. It kept her and Eileen going on bubble–gum and chews for weeks.

But now on Sunday afternoons there were the English visitors, and Noreen ran with Eileen, though her Daddy didn't like it much. Not so much because Eileen was a Catholic, he said – he liked to believe he wasn't that narrow – but because she was 'trouble', as he put it. She lived in one of the council houses on the new estate, which was the sort of place where people got drunk, and where old cars and motor-bikes roared at night. In Eileen's house grease still clung to breakfast dishes, and pork and crackling lingered, overpowering apple pie. Heaviness hung in air and bellies; Mr McAllister snored and Eileen's brother lazed, rude and arrogant, forcing his Ma to tears. She had to run back to her job in the hospital after lunch, and Noreen felt sorry for her, running from grease and dirt to sick and too much cleanliness. The men stayed heavy while the TV parroted, beer stank, and the girls ran.

They ran from the sordidness of Sunday, escaping along slow country roads, where couples pushed new babies in creaking prams and thrashed about old quarrels. The elderly nodded together, and dogs ran between their legs, mocking circles, or snuffled along behind like worn slippers, elderly too. Gangs of kids hid the other side of the dusty hedge, popping obscene mouths at Noreen and Eileen.

Boot boys shouted, 'Hey, wee doll!'

Noreen and Eileen stuck pouting lips in the air and marched on – but giggled.

'Wee doll! You're all right!'

They glanced at each other, abandoned poise, and ran, thrilled with Sunday, approved.

Sunday was a time for dressing up, more than anything: if you were a churchgoer, or if you were young.

Noreen's Ma had salvaged a white dress for her from the thrift shop in the barracks, where the Army wives brought old, unwanted clothes to make a bit of money out of them. Sometimes they weren't even old, quite new, in fact, but you could buy them for 50p just the same. So Noreen had a collection of strange hats, jumpers and skirts, of which she was very proud, and Eileen very jealous, although she pretended to scorn them. English people's ould clothes, indeed! But the white dress simply filled her with fury.

It had wee puff sleeves and a gently curving neckline,

then pink and blue smocking all the way down to the waist. The top part was tight-fitting, hugging Noreen's pertly developing body like a caress; then, from the tiny waist down, it flared out, luxurious, yet clung to her hips, which swung as she walked.

Eileen, in her years-old polyester skirt and flowered blouse, felt overshadowed and sulked beside the glowing Noreen, who was too delirious to care. For she had made the discovery, brought about by the white dress, that it was all right to show off her body.

It was that Sunday that the car stopped, a big white one with a smashed headlight and rust above the wheels. Noreen looked away quickly, kept her eyes fixed on the road ahead, but her face burned and there was a beating inside her skull. Suddenly she didn't feel powerful any more, and she wished she hadn't worn the clinging white dress.

Pop music bled from inside the car, and she was glad, for it muffled the thumping of her heart, which she could hear in her ears, very loud.

'Hey, beautiful!'

No one had ever called her that before. She dared a glance sideways and saw a dark, curly head and a hairy lip with a cigarette hanging from it. He grinned at her. She looked away again quickly. Laughter drowned the music.

'Want a spin, do you? Come on – don't be shy, now.'

That was a ginger-haired fellow in the back, with a pimply face. The driver was a tall, lean man, but you couldn't see what he was like, for he wore dark glasses.

A door swung open. Noreen was afraid. She bit her lip. 'Go away, won't you? We want to walk.'

'D'you hear that, Kenny? They want to walk.'

The voice in the car mocked her, and the fellows looked at Noreen's dress, every bit of it. Her face felt hot. The car frightened her – and angered her, even though she, with her tight, white dress, had enticed it. She looked at the pink, pocked face in the back.

'Get lost.'

Of course, she should have known that anger was the wrong thing (and didn't it say so in the Bible?). You only got more back. But she couldn't help it. She was angry.

'Fuckin' whore!' It was the ginger-haired one.

'Why not?' said another voice from the back. 'Sure don't you know her friend's a Fenian bitch?'

The car wheels spun, and Noreen's ears smarted.

'You and your white dress,' said Eileen, reproachful.

Noreen was miserable. She felt violated – for Eileen as well. She had humiliated them both, and was shocked.

'I'm sorry,' she said. 'They shouldn't call you that!' Then again, 'I'm sorry.'

'Ach, well, sure look at what they called *you*!' said Eileen. She grinned. 'Anyhow, you shouldn't have told them to go away. We could've had a rare spin.'

They both knew they wouldn't have dared, though. You had to watch it, or you'd get yourself a reputation, and then you'd had it. The boys all knew about you, and they'd gobble you up, spitting you out again when they'd finished, like a bit of old chewing-gum.

'Where d'you think they're away to?' Eileen's voice was wistful.

'Who?'

'Them fellows . . .'

Noreen blushed. 'Oh, they're away on into the town, I expect, to eye up the talent.'

'Or they could've gone to the sea,' said Eileen. 'Newcastle, maybe. That's where our Geraldine goes when she's courting. She goes on about it, you know: the bands playing on the sand, and how you sit eating fish and chips, or have a go on the amusements, or just sit watching everyone else.' She sighed.

'Then the dances,' said Noreen. 'I bet they go there . . . Or maybe they just drive the roads with the radio playing . . .'

They linked arms. They had forgotten the unpleasant side of the encounter already. They were both filled with a longing.

'Oh, Eileen! Wouldn't you just love to be bad, really bad!'

Eileen gave her a sideways look, then giggled. She fell silent.

'Wait, Noreen,' she said then. 'I have an idea . . .'

And that was when she spoke of the big dance at Ballynahinch, the first Friday evening in July.

'They would never let me go,' said Noreen, shaking her head. 'Never.'

They were slurping tea in Eileen's house. Michael had the radio on. 'My Dingaling' it was. It added to her depression somehow.

Of course her Da would never agree. He would say she was too young – barely fifteen – and doubtless it was some rough do: things like that. But she knew the real reason: it was that he saw it as part of the path to Hell – dancing, drinking – and, although he had no power over her heart, could not make her offer up her life to Jesus, he could at least still exercise some power over her physical being. He meant only good, but that didn't make it much easier to bear.

'Why tell them?' Eileen had said, draining her cup and twisting it round to see the tea leaves. She banged it down in the saucer as if something had been decided. 'Sure they need never know.' Noreen knew a delicious tingling of sin and pleasure and fear all mixed up together, like that first time, years ago when they mitched school together one fine day.

Even now she remembered the sensations so well: how she had stood outside the school, where she should have been, and heard 'All Things Bright and Beautiful' coming faintly from inside. It was the first time she had ever been bad, properly bad. (Eileen was, even then, a great persuader.)

At first she had been appalled at the thought of such sin, especially at the thought of being caught. 'My Da'd kill me!'

'Sure ould Des would never know! We'd pretend to go to school, of course, then meet round the other side of the hedge from the bus stop. And we'd have our sandwiches and all . . .'

And Noreen, impressed not least by Eileen's easy use of 'ould Des', was almost persuaded. Later, as she sat in her classroom at the top of the creaky stairs of the old white school, looking out of the window at the bare, beautiful Dromara hills, she was filled with an unbearable restlessness. She waited for Eileen's bus coming back from Lisburn that afternoon, after her own school was out. They agreed to go on the next good day.

When it came a few days later, Noreen didn't know whether to be pleased or not. She could tell it was fine by the strength of light coming in through her curtains while she still lay in bed. She had butterflies in her stomach, and when she got up she couldn't get her breakfast down. Ma looked at her and asked her was she all right? Not sickening for something, she hoped.

She dawdled up the road to school, still wondering about it, scuffing at stones with her shoes. She didn't have to go with Eileen, in theory at least. But the sun was hot already, between clouds, and the hills cut out clear against the blue sky through the hedge.

By the time she reached the school gates, all the other kids had gone in. The doors were closed, and after a bit she could hear them all singing in Assembly. A car passed by, a hum, and she walked on quickly round the corner to where Eileen was waiting by the hedge. You could see the sandwiches bulging in her cardigan pocket.

'Jesus, you took your time!' she said. 'Come on, now, let's get out of here quick, before someone sees us.'

For a moment Noreen considered running into school late, saying she'd overslept – anything; but Eileen was already walking off up the road. 'Come on!'

Noreen followed, feeling very conspicuous – anybody must know, just to look at them – but no one passed them, and the only sounds they could hear were the cows bellowing in McBrides' farm, as they came out from the milking.

She began to feel more hopeful. The sun shining filled them with that wonderful, carefree feeling that you could only have when you weren't in school, and they had their sandwiches besides.

They ran past the dirty, forbidden windows of Malcolm McDowell's old house, giggling, half afraid they might catch something. Mrs McAllister had told them about the old woman, the mother, who wore nothing but black, so it was said, since her husband died years ago; she hadn't been seen by anyone for yonks, though, so no one really knew whether she was still alive or not – not even Mrs McAllister, who knew everything about everyone.

Malcolm himself was a young, old man, with a blank, weather-creased face, big eager eyes like a child's. He must be turned forty now. All the kids used to laugh at him; they'd whoop and yell things at him, then run away, and the poor old fool was left standing there alone in the middle of the road, staring after them.

'Oh, Jesus, Mary and Joseph, there he is!' Eileen ran off with a screech, and Noreen followed, gasping. They slipped in through the wire and away down over the fields. Noreen looked back and she could see him: he was calling to them and waving with his large hands, and his bony knees tangled together like some gnarled tree that had been uprooted and blown by the wind. They ran on. The great piebald cows rushed off stifflegged, and the sheep scudded like clouds before them. But they were soon left behind, scattered, as Eileen changed direction and went running down a hill, with Noreen close behind. They were laughing and gasping when they reached the bottom.

Then they went hand in hand over fields that were cracked by bare stone walls, each one a mosaic of light.

They waded through quaggy fields and dark bogs brooding beneath angel hair of reeds, past ruins of old cottages where only sheep lived now. In some places the walls were merging back into the land from which they had once been taken, trampled by weather and animals. Rooks hung upside down from barbed wire that was tufted with sheep hair, sinister black corpses hung there by farmers to rot and frighten.

Up the crest of a hill, and there, on the other side, was the lough, lying blue in the fields, the edges tufted dun with reeds. Herons slid across it, grey ghosts, or stood in windows of water. Noreen and Eileen went slithering down steep banks, grabbing at reeds that tore their hands, down, down towards the silent, waiting water.

The cloudbanks came moving, muted, over the water, and the day turned mizzly, but it didn't matter. They poked about amongst the tadpoles that jelled and swayed at the edge of the lough, and sat down on one of the wooden jetties to eat their lunch. They dangled their legs over the edge and peered down into the ripples, but you could see nothing, only blackness. They shared their sandwiches, and all the while the rain misted down on them, studding their hair with diamonds.

Eileen told all about her brothers and sisters – one sister working in the rope factory, another married and living in the town, with a wee baby. Then there was Michael, who mitched off school and hung about Irwin's Garage instead. The people from the authorities kept coming round and pestering her Ma about it, but sure what could her Ma do? She'd still the weest one, Dermot, clinging to her apron anyhow. And her Da came in drunk and couldn't give a damn. He was drawing the brew for a while and that was awful, for he spent near all of it on the booze and then came home in a rage. They all had to be sure and keep out of his way then – he'd knock your head off. But now he had a regular job driving a van for some shop in the town, and things weren't so bad.

Noreen, whose Da was good-living and who had no brothers or sisters, listened in fascination. Once Noreen's Ma had nearly had another baby, but she had somehow lost it, too soon. Noreen only knew that it had been a wee girl (Ma didn't like to talk about it). A tiny, tiny wee girl.

She was silent. Eileen's arm crept through hers.

It happened as they stood up to go, brushing off crumbs and scrunching up greaseproof paper. Noreen's foot slipped from under her on the slimy boards, and she went down, ever so quietly it seemed, past the snails which clung to the green posts beneath the water, into a murky underworld of tendrils and debris.

Eileen, left behind on the jetty, invoked all the saints she knew of, and the dear Blessed Lady, and behold, it was mad Malcolm who came scrambling out of the bushes and waded into the water to hoke Noreen out.

'Jesus, what a stupid thing to do!' scolded Eileen, but she looked frightened. Her face glistened with rain, and Malcolm had a drip on the end of his red nose. Noreen couldn't stop coughing, and her clothes were plastered to her. Malcolm slowly took off his wet pullover from beneath his checked jacket, which was too short in the sleeves for him and covered with muck and hairs and God knew what else, and put it round her, for all the good it did.

He smiled at them benignly.

'Thanks,' said Eileen, and her own teeth chattered. 'Come on, Noreen, we'll be murdered! Thanks!' she yelled again. She gave Noreen a push, and they went away off across the stones, with Malcolm staring morosely after them. They began to run once they got into the field, and they were halfway up it before Noreen realized she still had Malcolm's smelly wet pullover round her.

'Ugh!' said Eileen. 'For God's sake, throw the ould thing away, Noreen!' They left it lying like a poor dead sheep beneath a hawthorn bush and ran on, giggling, though Noreen couldn't help remembering it later that night when she said her Lord's Prayer.

Noreen was soaked and convinced that she had swallowed a whole lot of fish. There would be no way of drying her off in time to go home, even were Mrs McAllister willing, and certainly no way of getting rid of the fish.

Of course, now the whole thing had to come out. Noreen's Ma and Da were furious, as was to be expected.

Ma dumped Noreen in the bath and the warmth creeping over her was lovely. Afterwards there was tea and hot buttered scones. Eileen was allowed some too, even though she hadn't fallen in the water. Da had just come back from one of his business trips on the mainland. There had been problems, and this was all he needed! He kept smoothing back his hair with his hand in an abstracted sort of way.

'I am surprised at you, Noreen,' he said to her quietly, shaking his head. 'Oh, I am surprised at you.'

It was only as she looked at his wounded expression

that she realized the enormity of what she had done. She had committed sin, she had spat in the Lord's face – not to mention in the faces of her parents – and now they would all, somehow, have to pay. She didn't dare look at him again. It was his silence that alarmed her most.

'Sure isn't she all right?' demanded Eileen. 'She's not dead or anything, like, Mr Logan.'

But Da just shook his head gravely. Of course Eileen could not understand, he said. She had missed the whole point, the whole point! Eileen fell silent and shrugged her shoulders.

Ma said that she'd always known there must be good in ould Malcolm, given the chance: he was just a bit gone in the head, that was all – and sure it wasn't his fault.

It was late afternoon by now, and Eileen went home for her tea. Her Ma never knew anything about the incident; nor would she have greatly cared, said Eileen. But Da gave Noreen passages from the Bible which she should read every evening before she went to bed. 'And,' he added quietly, but firmly, as was his way, 'you're to run wi' that one no more. No more!'

Ma sent Noreen off to school with a note which put her absence down to 'family troubles', and Noreen laboured conscientiously over the passages, which spoke of sin and repentance and redemption, but she knew that she could not possibly hold to her father's final commandment.

25

2

Eileen's sister Geraldine, who worked at the rope factory up the road, had posters of the Indians, the band who were to play at Ballynahinch, stuck inside her wardrobe door (in paint and full head-dress). She said that Eileen and Noreen might tag along with her and her fellow for the big dance. But she wouldn't take the blame for any bother, she said, eyeing Noreen and filing at her nails.

Eileen assured her that there would be no bother.

It was a miracle of planning. Ma would be at the Women's Institute that Friday, and Da would be in the Masonic Hall, where they all talked and had a big supper and other strange doings. There was a great air of secrecy surrounding those meetings, and Ma was painfully jealous of them, though she pretended not to be. Just a load of wee boys, she said, playing games. She was forever trying to persuade Da to tell her what they did, what went on, but he wouldn't give an inch. He never came in before two on those nights. It did annoy her.

But things went wrong from the beginning. Da didn't get in until seven o'clock, and then he'd to have his tea and get ready. He was running about looking for a clean shirt, with Ma running after him. As soon as he was out of the house, Ma sat down with a sigh of relief and started going on about the talk the women were going to have: about the pottery in Fermanagh, and how lovely it was, but expensive.

Noreen tried to show some interest, all the while wishing that she would just put on her coat and go.

'Will you be all right, now?' Ma asked at last, with her hand on the door. 'You know I don't like leaving you at night, Noreen . . . but I'll not be late back.'

'Oh, I'll be all right, don't worry your head about me. I'll maybe have an early night.'

Ma scrutinized her. 'Yes, you don't look so great,' she said. 'A bit pale. Mind you lock the door, now.'

You could hear her footsteps echoing in the yard, the gate squeaking, clanging. She was gone.

Before that first dance, Noreen stood in front of the big mirror in the bathroom and studied herself. She felt a certain guilt as she did it (didn't the Bible condemn vanity?), but she tingled under the remembered approval of boys: the way they looked at her, the things they called. It pleased her to think that she had 'looks', whatever these were; she had never really thought about it before, but suddenly it was important, more important than anything else.

She studied her face from all sorts of angles, trying to discover some new perspective which would disclose the secret of attractiveness. But there was only the face which she had always known: grey eyes, large like Da's (sometimes she felt, looking at him, as if she were looking into a mirror, and it made her uneasy, that she should be so like him), the nose short and tilted up at the end, long eyelashes. She closed her eyes and squinted through, trying to see what she would look like when some boy kissed her, but all she could see was a blur in the mirror. She combed her brown hair, which she washed once a week in beer to try and make it shine. One day she would get it cut, instead of letting it hang down around her face like a curtain: some posh, short style, all layered and flicked back, like the women in magazines. Ma was always saying what a mess it looked. She ran her hands through it to get it to sit up a bit more. It looked worse. She combed it again. A pimple on her chin. She frowned. A freckle that might pass for a beauty spot just above her lip.

Still, she liked what she saw: the way her waist had become slimmer, her hips fuller; most of all she liked the swelling of her breasts. They hadn't budded, like she'd read in books; they just sort of swelled up. It had been a very subtle, gradual process, and she'd tried to catch them growing, like you watch the hands of a clock for some barely perceptible movement, but they'd always managed to evade her.

She touched the soft hair between her legs, letting the fingers linger. Womanhood. An evocative word. Virginity was put on a pedestal. You'd to hold your legs close together in case it slipped out accidentally – a fragile crystal that would easily shatter. But it seemed to Noreen that not virginity, but this womanhood – her ovulating and menstruating and one day conceiving and bearing a child – that this was a state of almost mystic dimensions. It was something to do with those times when she sat huddled together with Eileen in the clothes press, sharing secrets; she remembered how it was warm and dark and safe, how it lulled you, and the cistern rumbled, like a belly. Well, one day she would be the warm, pulsating being; she would do the enclosing.

28

It was inside the womb of this cottage that the dark encounters of Noreen's life had taken place. That was how she thought of them: dark. Encounters of which she would never tell Ma. There had been sinister explorations with a spirit glass (better not to think of that; she shivered), and then other, shameful explorations, again with Eileen. She would rather not remember how they had touched and kissed in silent rooms (dirty, disgusting – Ma would say), and Eileen's breasts did bud like flowers. Yet it had seemed so natural, then; Eileen so soft and smooth . . .

But you learnt that there were things you did and did not do, and people with whom you did or did not do them. Their physical intimacy was finished now. They would not allow it, but pushed the idea away, along with other dark doings, which were tainted with the shame of sin, or abnormality, or unnaturalness – some such awful word, which made you shiver. They began saving their kisses and bodies for something else.

It was for this something else that Noreen told lies and ran off up the lane that first Friday evening, heart pounding, awkward in the platform shoes which she had picked up recently in the summer sales.

Ma had nearly gone spare when she brought them home, but Noreen loved them. They were white sandals with four-inch platforms – she had measured them, and they were four inches exactly, to her satisfaction. They made her look much taller, more elegant, she thought, especially with the long skirt. Ma had made that for the Christmas do at church, out of a piece of material she'd put aside for curtains and never used. It was a bit heavy but so pretty, with blue and white flowers. It took Ma only a couple of evenings to run it up.

She dabbed gold eyeshadow on her eyelids, blusher on her cheeks, and tried to cover up the spot with some peach-coloured stuff which she found in Ma's drawer. Next she had a go with the mascara. But she couldn't concentrate properly because of the butterflies in her stomach, and it kept smudging on to her cheek, so she'd to start all over again.

Looking at her watch, she discovered that it was gone nine o'clock already, and she was supposed to meet Eileen and Geraldine at nine. She rubbed the mascara off again and quickly lumped up the pillows in the bed to make it look as if there were someone in it (it couldn't fail, Eileen had said). She went through the cottage, being careful to lock the door and leave a couple of lights switched on. She took her jacket from its peg, stuffed her brush and make-up into the pocket, then opened her bedroom window and crept from her desk on to the ledge, scattering ornaments. She jumped down the other side, landing awkwardly in the clumpy shoes. She left the window just slightly ajar, and ran off into the dusk.

She couldn't rightly see the road in the half-light, and she swore as she tripped over stones. But glancing back at the neat rectangles of light that marked the cottage in the dark fields, she felt suddenly glad: glad because of her youth, her prettiness, her illicit freedom.

Her face was warm in the cool night as she ran all the way up the road until she came to the end of Westwinds Close. She saw a glowing fag-end of light in the dark, which was Geraldine, who wore a mock-fur jacket over her skirt.

'About time too,' she said crossly. 'We thought you were never coming.'

Noreen began muttering apologies.

'Ach, never mind all that!' said Eileen impatiently. 'Let's go, for God's sake! I can hear it coming!'

Sure enough, there was the groaning of the bus in the distance. They ran for all they were worth up to the crossroads and just made it, scrambling up the steps as it was drawing away, spilling out their coins to the driver. Noreen had never been on the late night bus before, and she noticed the stale smell of toilets and cigarettes. There were only two other passengers, a middle-aged woman wearing a headscarf that had riding whips on it – she was clutching a plastic shopping bag and yawning, almost nodding off as the bus started again – and a drunk half-way down the bus, sprawled over two seats. He stared at them with bleary eyes as they swung past and made a half-hearted grab at Geraldine's jacket, but she pulled away from him angrily. They all collapsed together in the back seat, their chests heaving with the running.

Geraldine began examining her stockings, which were all mud-spattered. 'They were new on tonight, sweet Jesus!' She lit another cigarette, blew out the smoke in a long stream and sat looking out of the window into the dark, legs crossed.

Eileen, who'd been hoping for a cigarette too, shrugged her shoulders. She'd put her long red hair up in a bun, but it was all coming down round her face now, with the running, and Noreen fixed it for her with difficulty.

'What were you so late for?' She was cross now, with her hair ruined, and spots of rain on the window too.

The bus swung and jerked round corners in the night, past distant rectangles of light across fields, and Noreen felt suddenly dejected, sitting there with Geraldine and Eileen who were silent, and the leering drunk and the tired-eyed woman in the headscarf, on the old bus that smelt.

She looked at her watch: twenty five to ten. Ma would be home now from the school, sitting before the TV. Noreen wished for a minute that she were there too.

They spilled out of the bus in Dromora, where Geraldine's fellow, Barry, met them. He was tall and tight-jeaned, with shoulder-length, feathered hair. He looked like a pop star. Eileen grinned at him, and Geraldine, running her fingers through her dyed blond curls, frowned at her.

It was gone ten o'clock by now, but there were lots of people about, gangs of fellows and couples, entwined, all making for the bar across the road. You could hear a great noise coming from it, glasses and shouting and music. Cars were raking up and down the street.

'Drink?' asked Barry, rubbing his hands with the cold and the prospect.

'Sure how can we,' replied Geraldine, 'wi' them.' She nodded her head towards Noreen and Eileen, wrinkling her nose slightly.

'We don't mind,' said Eileen. 'Do we, Noreen?'

'I'm not getting into trouble because of yous! Well,' she conceded, 'you might pass for something like eighteen, just, but her, never!'

Noreen's face burned. She looked at the ground. The

rain was coming on again, and people were running for the bar.

'Ach, leave the wee girl alone,' said Barry, shifting from one foot to another. 'Sure it doesn't matter. We'll head on.'

They squeezed into his van, which said DEVLIN - ELECTRICS on it. The engine roared and they were soon out of the town. They drove along dark, tree-lined lanes, and needles of rain caught in the headlights through the windscreen wipers which were creaking and clacking. Noreen and Eileen had to sit on the floor in the back, along with some old ropes and a crate of rattling bottles which kept sliding towards them whenever they went round a corner.

Barry stopped to pick up some fellow who was thumbing a lift, with his leather jacket pulled up over his head.

'Brendan.'

'Barry. How about you, boy?'

'Oh, all right. You know Geraldine, and this is Eileen, and –'

'Noreen.'

'Ach, yes, Noreen.'

'Hiya.' Brendan grimaced and sat squashed between Noreen and Eileen in the back. The rain dripped off him on to their skirts and he kept blowing his nose into a great striped handkerchief.

'Have yous been to the dance before?' He had to yell above the noise of the engine.

'No,' said Noreen.

'No,' Eileen added quickly. 'We usually go to the dance in Banbridge.' Noreen looked at her, and her face was quite straight.

Eileen and Brendan talked the rest of the way, and Noreen was glad when they arrived.

You could see the lights of the hotel, which was set back off the road. The car-park was already full, and they had to park in the road a few hundred yards back. They walked up through the dark, and it was a shock to go in through the doors into the bright light. A man standing just inside the door took their money and stamped their hands. Noreen discovered that she didn't have quite enough, and Geraldine paid for her with a sigh. Then they went on into the main hall, where the lights were dimmed and the first band was playing.

This was it, then. Noreen stood close by the others, taking it all in. At the moment the place was mainly full of girls who lined the walls like poor, dried-up sunflowers hoping for water. They talked to each other behind their hands and giggled, and waited. Gradually the hall filled up with the fellows, who came in from the bars, rolling a bit as they brushed past you, staring, and you could smell the beer on them. One nudged another as they went past Noreen, said something which she couldn't hear above the music. They both laughed.

Some of the girls were dancing together now, while the fellows stood about in bunches, joking and belching, whistling occasionally, but still they were reluctant to approach.

Geraldine and Barry were already entwined together somewhere in the ocean of the dance-floor, and Brendan, who wore tight checked trousers and a college jumper, asked Eileen to dance. Noreen was left alone. She was alarmed all of a sudden, finding herself adrift in the sea of nameless bodies and unfamiliar noise. She was heading for the safety of the loos, when a dark, curly-haired fellow stepped in front of her.

It was the boy who had stopped that Sunday in the white car. Kenny. She'd heard his name that day.

'Dance?' he demanded, swaying slightly, trying his best to focus swimming eyes on her face. She was sure she could see the alcohol in them – deep brown pools of burning alcohol. They were lovely.

'All right, then.' It was easier, somehow, because he was drunk, and didn't notice her embarrassment, didn't know how inexperienced she was. He took her hand – his was moist and warm – and led her to the dance-floor, where they fought their way between pleached couples and managed a few rounds of the hall before that song ended and another began. As the first band packed up and the Indians were announced, the crowd was so tight she could hardly breathe. Kenny's arm was round her. There was deafening applause as they ran on with their painted faces and headbands, dark hair streaming down their backs. She would never forget it, never. Jokes at the microphone, more applause, then 'The Black Hills of Dakota', 'Running Bear', 'And I Love You So'. Noreen would never forget it, as she was shoved and whirled through the fairground of Friday night.

Then there was 'I Lay Beneath the Blanket on the Ground', and Kenny took her hand and led her back through the crowd. They had no blanket, but made do with one of the benches that lined the walls of the hall. He lay on top of her, sluggish with alcohol, and although she thought she loved him already, she wished he weren't so heavy.

Then he was busy with his clumsy explorations, getting under her blouse, her skirt, heedless of the other couples staggering against them and of the old men leering from the loos.

At last the frantic fumbling stopped, and he lay quiet. Noreen was relieved – what her mother would have said – but somehow, she didn't feel any danger with him. Shyly, she pushed her fingers through the dark curls of his hair, stroked his clothes. It was the first time she had ever done this to a boy, and he felt rough: Eileen's hair was fine and soft, like Ma's lamb's-wool cardy.

Kenny was different. Different from the boys in school too, who were all young, combed and surely utterly without passion; nor was he like the boot boys, shorn and large-footed, with spikes that hurt. Kenny smelt of manhood – or alcohol, at least. Noreen was inebriated with him, and with his touch, the dancing, the haze of dim lights, the twanging music. This was excitement, the life which her adolescence demanded of her, the experience she craved. Surely it was.

And the highlight of all the euphoria was, without doubt, 'The Sash', the song which celebrates the victory of Protestant over Catholic, which Kenny and his friends started singing at the end. Soon others were joining in. The Indians had sung their last songs, made their bows, signed a few books – Noreen glimpsed Geraldine up there. Now the dancers sang their own song. This was what made it a proper night out.

> It is old but it is beautiful,
> And the colours they are fine,
> It was worn in Derry, Aughrim,
> Enniskillen and the Boyne.

> Sure me father wore it in his youth
> In the grand old days of yore,
> And it's on the Twelfth I love to wear
> THE SASH ME FATHER WORE!

They all shouted the last line and it was great. A patriotic frenzy gripped all those fervent, Protestant hearts: the drunken lads, the giggling girls in long skirts, the middle-aged adulterers, the leering old men. Every one of them joined hands and sang their hearts out in a big circle.

In the middle of it all, Noreen was dimly aware of someone pulling at her, and she turned reluctantly to find Eileen.

'We're going,' she said, and Noreen, drunk with excitement, couldn't understand why she was so grim.

'But why? Not yet, Eileen!'

'We're not staying for this! Are you coming, or not?'

She couldn't go now, not now. The people were all dancing and singing, and Kenny grabbed her arm, so that she was back in the circle again, tossed around the room.

She saw the fellows approach out of the corner of her eye, not fully understanding. The next minute they had Kenny by the jacket; it didn't take much, for he was already unsteady with the drink, and when they hit him he simply crumpled up, very slowly and surprisingly gracefully, then thudded heavily on to the floor.

The singing had stopped. There was shouting as the circle broke up, and a girl screamed. Kenny's ginger-haired mate was coming forward, face contorted, but the bouncer was there before him. Already you could hear a police siren in the distance. Couples were making for the door, and the band was hastily packing up on stage. Chairs were overturned and a light bulb smashed. In the middle of the chaos, Noreen glimpsed Geraldine and Barry going out the door together, followed by Eileen, who was pulling on Brendan's arm. Brendan spat contemptuously on the floor, and the door swung to behind them.

The police arrived, and the hall cleared quickly. A few lads were led off, cursing. One kicked at Kenny, who was still unconscious, with his Doc Marten as he went by. Kenny stirred slightly at this point. His eyes half-opened, flickered, then he turned on his side and vomited.

'There's true love for you,' said the lad, and went off laughing.

One of the policemen hauled Kenny to his feet and sat him on a bench at the side of the hall. 'You all right, love?' he asked Noreen.

She nodded, biting her lip. He went, and she was left alone with her wretched partner in the empty dance-hall. There was no magic now. The cruel glare of a stark bulb stripped the place of any illusions it might have tried to prolong. The floorboards were bare, the walls cold and scarred. Chairs lay on their sides, defenceless and broken. A plastic fan gaped on the wall. Cans and bottles littered the floor amongst the vomit and fag-ends.

There was a step behind Noreen. It was the bouncer, a fat man with greasy lips.

'D'you want a lift home, love?' he asked her, with his eyes on her blouse. 'Sure thon's no use to you! Thon's a shocking way to treat a girl.' He moved closer, and he

smelled of sweat. 'I'll give you a lift.' Kenny was staggering to his feet.

'No. No thanks.'

The bouncer swore at her and the door slammed
behind them, Kenny leaning on her arm. The car-park
was empty, and there were no lights, save a single dim
one somewhere inside the dance-hall. It was quiet, eerily
quiet – she'd never been out so late before – only a car
roaring in the distance, fading. They started off down
the road, which echoed with their footsteps. He was
leaning heavily on her. She couldn't see how this night
would ever end. (Why, oh why, hadn't she gone with
Eileen?)

Kenny left her, with difficulty, at a small crossroads
near the dance-hall. He managed to kiss her, leaning by
a humpbacked bridge, then swayed, hiccuped, righted
himself again.

'Jesus fuckin' Christ.' He looked at her and grinned
slowly. 'Be seein' you,' he said then, and disappeared
into blackness. All Noreen could hear was the stumbling
of heavy feet against stones. A belch.

She was alone.

She hoped she was going the right way. She'd no way
of knowing. She just kept walking.

A dog howled with the night, somewhere far off; it
echoed in her blood, which rushed in her ears. She
thought, someone is about to die, or has died. Shivered.
there was a rustling in the long grass on the other side of
the scrubby hedge. She stopped walking and crouched
down. Heavy breathing. She could just make out two
dark eyes staring into hers. She wanted to scream, but
couldn't, then didn't. It was a cow. A bloody cow. She

walked on more lightly after that, took off her platform shoes to make it easier. Surely only she, of all the people in the world, was walking on the black, exposed disc that constitutes the earth. Only she existed.

The rain came, drenching the long skirt, and her stockinged feet sloshed through puddles (oh, if only she'd gone with Eileen!). She thought she must be walking to the end of the world.

Then the moon flew free and bright again, splitting the clouds. It silvered a cold stream which gushed beneath a stone bridge, and the colours of the stone glimmered. They were painted red, white and blue, and across the road was scrawled in stark, white letters: NO SURRENDER.

The streetlights shone in the puddles on the main road. There was no rain now, no cars. It was ghostly. The moon lit up the wee road and was reflected too in the dark windows, the mockery of a face. All dark except one. Noreen was about to hoist herself in through the bedroom window, when she hesitated, went on down the yard to the sitting-room window. The curtains weren't quite drawn, and she could see, by the dim light of the brass tablelamp in the corner, Ma sitting on the sofa in her dressing-gown and mules, head down on her chest as if she were asleep, but her eyes were open.

Ma looked up slowly as Noreen quietly opened the door and stood there. The skirt clung to her and the twisted white platform shoes were in her hand. Ma looked her up and down, and Noreen thought, it can't really be happening.

'And where in God's name have you been?' Ma's anger was quiet, but loaded; her lips hard. She frightened Noreen more than Da, somehow.

Noreen glanced at the clock. Twenty five past four. She was so tired. So tired. 'I missed my lift.' That was pointless. Her bottom lip quivered. All she wanted was to be in bed.

'You must think I'm stupid,' said Ma bitterly. 'Stupid.'

Noreen shook her head hopelessly.

'Why did you not ask?'

'You wouldn't have let me go.'

'I didn't know what to do,' Ma went on. 'Whether to call the police, set out looking for you . . .'

Noreen had nothing to say. There was a creaking of boards in the attic; the house at night. She couldn't see, seriously, how her life would ever go on again. It would surely stop here, on Friday, the second of July, and never start again.

'I'm disgusted at you,' said Ma. 'A daughter of mine –'

There was the roar of the car down to the gates, the door slamming, the garage door.

'There's your Da,' said Ma. Then, 'Ach, get away to bed. We'll discuss it in the morning. Go on!'

Noreen crept off, leaving Ma sitting on the sofa, relieved that she wouldn't have to face Da that night, at least. She heard Da's footsteps down to the door, and then she thought she could hear their voices. She peeled off the wet clothes and fell asleep almost as soon as she got into bed. But then she woke up some time in the still dark, early hours, with everything going round in her head, while Saturday's grey dawn made ghosts of the furniture in the wee room.

3

She woke up to the awful knowledge that this time there would be no forgiveness: not like after the stealing. Then it had seemed that there was a fresh trust between them afterwards, a sort of renewal, born of the pain of the thing.

It had happened after she'd been in McCauley's with Eileen one day after school. They'd had a blow out: two cream buns each, and only 5p left between them. Feeling giddy with gluttony and rather sick, they headed for Willis's to fill in the time before the bus came. They looked at the make-up, and Eileen pinched a few sweets which they munched on their way round, despite the cream buns.

Then they wandered through the clothes section, and it was there that Noreen spotted the lovely slim gold belt. Well, it wasn't really gold, but it glittered and sparkled just the same, hanging on its stainless-steel rail. Noreen tried it on and looked in the mirror; and then she knew that she could do nothing else but pocket the thing. She couldn't possibly leave it behind, for by the time she'd the money saved up, it was bound to have been sold. It was a cinch to fold it up and slip it into her pocket, but it was the biggest thing she'd ever taken, and by the time they got to the glass exit doors, she was blushing furiously, convinced that everyone could see the bulge in her blazer pocket.

And then there was the hand on her shoulder. 'I believe you have something in your pocket.'

She turned. She saw a thick-set woman with large teeth and pale lips, her grey hair combed back. She wore a plucked grey skirt and a light blue twinset with a white diamond pattern, which was wrong in one place and had blue where there should have been white. Noreen kept her eyes on it as the woman led her through the shop and knocked on a door at the far end. She spoke in a low voice to the man inside and then went, smiling at Noreen like a dying nightmare. Old cow.

The man told Noreen to come in, wearily. He wore a brown suit and glasses and suggested that Noreen empty her pockets. She almost giggled, despite the seriousness of the situation, but did as he said, and very soon there was an assortment of crumpled paper bags, dirty hankies and some old chewing-gum on the table. She felt a bit embarrassed about the gum, all grey and wrinkled. It should have been stuck under some desk somewhere. And at last came the coveted, guilty belt, only its gold no longer seemed to sparkle. Indeed, it looked blatantly artificial now, rather vulgar, and Noreen wondered why on earth she'd bothered.

The man looked at her with an expression of resignation, or perhaps boredom, and asked her age.

'Fourteen.'

'Old enough to take responsibility for your actions, then.'

Responsibility. That was the sort of thing her father would have said. Noreen followed the patterns on the lino floor, round and round and along and up under the filing cabinet; but when she came back, the man was still looking at her expectantly, and the wretched belt still sat on his desk along with the ancient chewing-gum. She sighed.

That seemed to spark something off in him. This was how delinquents began, he informed her: first it was sweets, make-up and small items of clothing; in a few years' time, it would be a bank!

What crap. It wasn't like that at all, she wanted to explain: not criminal, like. This now was just some funny sort of urge or kick, and she didn't really mean any harm. It was the divil in her. But what was the use? She looked at the floor again.

He finished up saying she'd probably learnt her lesson, and he'd give her the chance to do the right thing: tell her parents about what she'd done. Otherwise, it would have to come from him, and that would be much worse.

She had to write down her name, address and telephone number on the piece of paper which he shoved towards her. It never occurred to her to give a false one.

She was young yet, he said then, and maybe she'd been caught in time. But if he ever saw her in this shop again . . .

Noreen didn't wait to hear any more. She fled the room, dodging through the shoppers and past the check-point at the door, to find a rather cross Eileen leaning against the wall outside.

'What did you go and get caught for?' she demanded, as if Noreen had done it on purpose, for God's sake. She raised her eyes heavenwards and popped a sweet in her mouth. Then they heard the bus coming up the road and had to run for it, and ended up missing the back seat.

In the end she hadn't the nerve to tell. Her parents trusted her, see. She mooned about all weekend, didn't go out with Eileen, as was their custom, but sat down by the stream, where years ago she'd made a house of gorse and been good.

Then, on the Monday night it came. All that business with Da. She didn't like to think about it much – how she'd failed with him. After he left, shutting the door quietly behind him, she turned out the lamp and lay on the bed in darkness, apart from the moon, which tore through the flimsy curtains and shivered on the floor.

At breakfast time there was Ma, tight-lipped and pale. She didn't say much, only that she was disappointed, but no doubt it wouldn't happen again. If Noreen wanted something so much . . .

But then Noreen caught sight of her wet eye, and was in her arms. They hugged each other for dear life, and Noreen felt the softness of the lamb's-wool cardy against her skin, Ma's warmth against hers. At last Ma touched her shoulder and went to get ready for work.

So saved, forgiven, graced with new intimacy – with Ma, at least – Noreen renounced Willis's. That particular sin had no more power. The penitent waited outside while Eileen went in to look at the make-up and clothes. There was still McCauley's, for a wholesome milk shake and a wicked cream bun. And, above all, there were still Sundays.

She held on to that, during the awful weekend of the dance, when Ma and Da closed her, with their reproaches, out of their world. Or rather – and this knowledge was worse – she, with her deceit, had closed herself out of it. She knew now that nothing would ever be quite the same again between them.

She waited for Sunday afternoon, when at least she would have the comfort of Eileen's company, as they walked the roads, arm in arm. But when she arrived at the McAllisters' that Sunday, Eileen wasn't there. The house was a mess: Mrs McAllister rushing about with piles of clothes and searching cupboards for things, while Mr McAllister sat in front of the TV with a glass of beer, quite oblivious to the frenzy around him.

Mrs McAllister seemed almost surprised to see Noreen. 'She's away out,' she shouted above the commercial, 'wi' Geraldine and some friends . . .'

'Oh.' Noreen felt put out. She and Eileen never missed a Sunday, never. Surely Eileen wouldn't hold Friday night against her? It was then that she remembered guiltily how she had sung 'The Sash' that night, pulled along by Kenny and the rest. Eileen's face had been grim as she went out the door. But there was no harm in it, surely. It was just a song to sing along with everyone else, a way of belonging. She had never really thought about what it meant.

Noreen was conscious of Mrs McAllister's eyes on her. 'When would she be back, then?' Her own voice sounded strange, small to her.

'I really couldn't say, Noreen.' The unaccustomed coldness in Mrs McAllister's voice almost hurt her with a physical pain. 'We're going away on holiday tomorrow, you know,' she went on, 'down South – so she'll not be here for a while, now.'

'Oh.' Noreen turned to go. She'd always felt at ease here, like one of the McAllisters, almost. She'd shared their tea many afternoons, played crackly records with Eileen, been scolded by Mrs McAllister as if she were her own mother. But now something had been withdrawn from her in this house too. She had the feeling of having sinned, fallen from grace – from her parents' grace, from the McAllisters' grace. All that remained was a dreadful sense of loss, as if something had died.

Mrs McAllister made as if to say something, then changed her mind. Noreen took her leave quickly, aware of Mrs McAllister standing by the front window, looking after her, a great pile of clothes in her arms. The gate clanged behind her, an empty, echoing sound.

Her Da was relieved that she wasn't running with Eileen any more; she'd been on a wrong track there. Perhaps now, he said, things would be better. He asked her if she would go to the Young Evangelicals – just one meeting, to see. She seemed to have lost direction, he said.

Sometimes, when they used to go to Granny Logan's for tea on Sunday afternoons, she would come upon Da and Granny sitting in some corner, leaning forward to each other in earnest conversation, knees almost touching. Granny's grey, wiry curls shook as she whispered; now and then she half turned her head to make sure no one could overhear them, and Noreen knew they were talking about Granda, who watched the football on Sundays instead of going to church (she wondered if they talked about her too, and Ma).

They even prayed for him in the Meeting once. Poor Granda. Noreen had listened with a strange mixture of horror and fascination as the born-again prayed for the souls of their beloveds, for their friends and relatives who were not saved, but doomed to burn in the eternal fires of Hell. Granny Logan's veined eyelids were shut tight as her quavering voice pleaded with the Lord for the lost soul of her dear husband, Maurice. Ma, who was sitting beside Noreen that night, had given her a strange look. Noreen preferred the nights when she and Ma left Da to go on to the Meeting alone, which often happened when she was only wee. As they tramped home together from the church, the dusk bled a tangerine stain across the naked hills, making the sky glow wonderfully.

She held Ma's hand tight as the cars swooped by, lighting up the bogey men in the hedges, and the council houses hid, sinister, behind their concrete walls. Past Isabel's shuttered shop, where the petrol sign hung like a dead man, then they turned off down the road into utter blackness, leaving behind the orange sky, which filled Noreen with a lostness and an obscure fear.

Then home, the hum of the garden gate and the dog whining in the warm kitchen, slobbery tongue wet on her bare hands and legs. Ma bustled about the kitchen, coatless, but with her Sunday hat still on – a fawn hat, which was soft like an animal, with a velvet band round it. Warm milk and sandwich and bed, dreaming at the bright crack in the curtains. She never heard Da come in on those nights.

But then later, when she was older, it was expected of her – Da expected it of her – that she should go to the Meeting along with the others. The Meeting was held in the Evangelical Mission Hall which stood in the fields like a cowshed and was painted green. Here all the men and women and some of the older children came every Sunday evening to sing His praises to the wailing accompaniment of an electric organ, which was played by a young fellow with pale ginger hair and thin arms. All dressed-up to the hilt they'd be, the women with their hats and bags, the men in polished shoes and swept hair, the kids in tapping shoes and buttoned coats.

There was always a great crowd, so that you had to park on the verge and then push your way in through all the ones standing about, blethering in the raw dark outside the bright hall. They were stomping and rubbing and blowing, and you could see their breath hanging in the frosty air. The Meeting belonged to winter, somehow, for Noreen; her only memories of it were of that time of constant semi-darkness, when you weren't quite sure you were living.

In the hall, a bare, bright bulb dangled from the ceiling, and a electric fire glowed dull orange at the front. You sat in rows on wooden benches that made your backside sore, and the leader sat at a big table at the front. He was a large man, with white hair swept back and teeth like yellowed tombstones. His voice soared out over his hymn-book and hovered over them all near the ceiling somewhere. The congregation sat meekly whilst the Reverend McConaghy castigated them for being sinners, and told them how they would go to Hell unless they accepted God's wonderful gift, which was Eternal Life through Jesus Christ our Lord. They must repent, they must be born again, they must be saved. He pointed the finger, and Noreen quivered in her seat.

Sometimes there were visiting speakers who told

stories and showed slides, and you had tea and buns afterwards. Once it was some great Ulster crusader speaking about the mission in Brazil, and one man with a big bloated face went off to sleep – right in the front row he was too – with his arms folded and his blubbery lips open. Ma said that it was only Jimmy, who had a speech defect and other things besides, and he couldn't help it, poor ould crittur. Anyhow, the crusader gave no sign of having noticed, and afterwards there were scones and brack and wee fairy buns with pink icing, which Ma had made. There was a fair turnout that night, and they didn't get anything left to take home with them.

Then the drive home, shivering on the cold car seat, and Da driving slowly because of the black ice on the roads, crawling the bends.

One night, as they drove home, there was a red point of light in the darkness, and Noreen's stomach turned as the car skidded, then stopped. The soldiers in their camouflage surrounded the car. They made Da switch out the headlamps, and one of them shone in a torch, which dazzled Noreen. He asked them where they had been, where they were going, and then he made them turn round and go another way. He looked in the boot too, but there was nothing interesting, only her Da's tool box and an old rope.

They turned round and set off on another road, and it was then that Noreen first saw the place where the sun went down. She was shocked. That sunset had been coming from here all along, she saw now – the many many lights, the low bunkers and the barbed wire surrounding it all. There were wooden look-out huts up high, and she glimpsed a face in one of them. She must be looking into Hell, she thought.

'That's where they put the bad boys,' said her Da, confirming her suspicions, and she was afraid suddenly of his forehead, which she could see stippled with the lights in the car mirror, for she didn't know whether she was saved or not.

The Young Evangelicals met every Saturday night in young Paul Megarry's house (young, they called him – but he was at least twenty-two). It was the sort of thing which the girls in school would have mocked her for, if she'd let on: Jesus people, freaks – it was so unfashionable. In school you couldn't be seen saying the Lord's Prayer in Assembly, or you were labelled wet or a swot, some such awful thing.

That Saturday night, Noreen sat shy and sceptical and cross-legged on a cushion on the floor in the room full of singing young people. You were all crammed in together, and whenever the singing stopped or there were prayers, you were afraid your stomach would rumble. The only person she knew was wee Jimmy McCormack, who used to go to the village school with her. He lived in the big white house beside the cemetery, and once he was walloped with Ryan's battered slipper before the whole school in Assembly, after the prayers.

Noreen had felt sorry for Jimmy, but she giggled along with all the rest; later she prayed that it would never happen to her. She tried to make a pact with God: if He would only stop It happening, then she would always believe in Him and try to be good; she'd say her prayers every day and stop eating sweets in Assembly. But He gave no sign of having heard.

Eileen was all right, of course; she went to something called confession, where she told all the wrong things she'd done to a priest, then said Hail Marys and was forgiven. They didn't have anything like that in Noreen's church, unfortunately.

Jimmy McCormack wasn't wee any more, of course; he was tall now and his lean face earnest looking. He was a born-again Christian, people said. It was no wonder, really, for someone who lived beside the cemetery and whose Ma never let him play with other kids.

He went down the bus sometimes on the way home from school, handing out wee bits of paper, which made everyone giggle awkwardly. Away in the head, was that Jimmy! When you stopped giggling and sneaked a glance (you didn't like to be seen doing it), the bits of paper would invite you to the Mission Hall to hear some reverend or other speak. There would be a talk and slides – about the work in Brazil or Africa, wherever – and afterwards coffee and biscuits. As if that would attract anybody! Noreen always screwed the bit of paper up and stuffed it in her pocket; she didn't like to just drop it on the floor, like some of the others did. Jimmy must have noticed, for he nobbled her once, getting down off the bus.

'You'll come, won't you, Noreen?'

'Oh, I hardly think it.'

His face fell, but he tried again. 'Why not? Sure you'll never know what it's all about, if you don't come along. You have to at least give these things a chance.'

'Well, I'm busy, you know, Jimmy.' She glanced at him sideways. 'Thanks all the same.'

'No one's ever too busy for God,' said Jimmy quietly. 'He won't take that as an excuse on the Day of Reckoning. Think of that, Noreen!'

He spoke like one of those placards which old men in raincoats carried round the streets of Belfast. 'Now is the time!' they proclaimed. 'Be saved, before it is too late!' They went on about sin and condemnation and Hell, and people laughed at them, with their predictions of doom. They had no time for damnation; life was trouble enough.

What was it then, to be saved? Oh, she'd always known about it, of course – conversion. The red, religious letters nailed to the trees warned you. 'Call ye upon the Lord!' they commanded. 'Repent, and be saved!' It was the same in church on Sundays and in the Meeting. Noreen looked upon it all as a great bore, and yet it disturbed her in some indefinable way which she didn't like to admit, even to herself. She worried – just very occasionally the thought crossed her mind – about what would happen afterwards.

Being saved, Noreen concluded, was all about stopping doing things. That was how it seemed. You stopped drinking, smoking, dancing – you turned good-living, like Da. It had happened to him when he was a young man, one night in a Meeting – but it never happened to Ma, and this caused him great sadness.

Noreen wasn't sure what she believed – apart from in a sort of darkness. Once she had been to the Catholic chapel with Eileen, and there she had found a veiled softness in the ceremony, the incense, the robed priest, the chanting . . . You could lose yourself in all that. It had drawn her, with its promise of something hidden, magical, something dark. She could believe in a God like that.

But the Protestant Church was dry, the light too bright in her own religion. You felt that here was something that seared and cut, divided: good or bad, saved or damned, Heaven or Hell. It couldn't be that simple. For Ma was not bad; no, she was lovely and warm and good, yet she was not saved, and so would go to Hell. Noreen couldn't believe that. But they told you that it was all to do with grace and faith, rather than goodness; and anyway, God had His own reasons for doing things, which mere humans couldn't hope to understand. They had to just follow blindly, have faith, even if they didn't know what in.

Yet the Young Evangelicals sang and some of their faces glowed. They prayed, searching their hearts, sincerely, especially one girl, whose long brown hair fell forward to hide her face like a prayer curtain. A solemn boy with thick glasses shared a verse from the Bible, which he said the Lord had laid upon his heart, and the fellow sitting beside him on the couch pressed his knees together and blushed. There were about fifteen of them altogether, all well dressed, the boys in good trousers and shirts and pullovers, the girls in skirts and tights. They gave the impression of being very clean, somehow.

And then there was Paul. A tall, dark fellow, with a quivering point of nose and a gentle voice. Dark wavy hair and a moustache. He played the guitar and sang softly, songs of love to Jesus. He spoke of Jesus' love, and Noreen had never heard anyone speak like that before; not of love (the sort of thing that most people giggled at). Paul spoke of it unashamedly, yet gently – Jesus, friend, lover, comforter, the one to give your life meaning. Noreen looked down. It was embarrassing.

Afterwards there were coffee and sandwiches and buns, which a smiling Mrs Megarry brought in on a trolley. The young people stood about talking earnestly and smiling and munching. The brown-haired girl, Rosalind, came and chatted to Noreen about this and that – where she lived, where she went to school, and then she asked her, was she saved?

'I don't think so,' said Noreen.

Rosalind nodded sympathetically, and then it was time to go.

Paul took her hand between his large, shapely ones as she was going out the door. 'You'll come again, Noreen, won't you?'

His blue eyes were gentle and piercing and bright all at once; she thought he must be able to see right into her. She was glad to be away from there that night.

4

On Thursday the sun shone, for it was the Twelfth of July. Noreen was going to the parades.

Her Da was in a rare holiday mood, wearing his light cord trousers and a checked shirt that was open at the neck. The factory was closed – all the firms took the Twelfth fortnight, for it was the biggest holiday of the year, apart from Christmas, perhaps; but King Billy marched through the streets in a way that Christ never did.

Everything stopped on the Twelfth, and it seemed that the sun always shone on that day; the roads were crawling with cars, all on their way to see the parades. Of course, you couldn't get anywhere near the middle of the town; the police were there, directing everybody to park in a field on the outskirts, and then you had to walk on up into the centre, past last night's bonfires which were still smouldering in places.

Union Jacks waved in the streets and were splashed along the kerbs; King Billy watched the proceedings, of which he was the main part, from the walls of houses. It was blazing hot already. Noreen, dressed in her best jeans and blouse, tingled with the first drums, as she waited amongst screaming children and harassed mothers and other, tight-jeaned girls like herself, impatient for the first glimpse of boys and bands and boyfriends.

Then, as the bands turned a corner somewhere further down the town, you could suddenly hear them, thin but clear, and everyone cheered. They came gradually nearer, sometimes louder, then fainter for a moment, as they made their way up through the town. And then, at last, you could see them, a blur of blue and black in the distance, until you were marching too.

Oh, it was grand, the Twelfth!

First came the wee baton boy, dancing about across the street, throwing and twirling his baton with such nonchalance – behind his back, between his legs, spinning up in the air, then caught by a little finger. Then the big drum heading all the others – the drums and flutes and accordions, all the men resplendent in their shiny uniforms. It was the flutes that Noreen loved best: they sounded high and light above the steady, rhythmic beat of the drums, making your heart sing. The fellows were all concentrating with pursed lips, and they were lovely in their black trousers and blue jackets. There was gold braid on the sleeves, and a feather waved from each blue beret. One fellow grinned at Noreen as they passed: he had dark, curly hair and the beginnings of a moustache. She smiled back, breathless suddenly, for it was him – Kenny. She glanced round quickly, but her parents had disappeared in the crowd somewhere. Then, all too soon, the bands with their bright colours were gone, shimmering round the corner, and the flutes grew faint. There were only the silent Orangemen, sombre in their dark suits and bowler hats; they carried umbrellas even in this weather and wore orange sashes. Their eyes were hard.

They marched along to a single drum: a thud, thud, which made you shudder as you looked at their dark faces. They introduced another element into all the gaiety, a strangely sinister element which, just for a moment, made you stop and wonder. Yet they were part of the tradition, a tradition which Noreen had observed unthinkingly ever since she was small. She could recall many Twelfth days when she held Ma's hand in the sunshine, wearing her shorts and clutching a half-eaten ice-cream, as the bands went by. But today she felt a sudden sense of betrayal towards Eileen, even though she reasoned with herself that really it didn't matter; it was only a bit of fun.

Then she found herself remembering another time. It was years ago now, when Ma had taken her to look for clothes in a factory shop in some place near the border, where you couldn't drive your car through the town. It was one Saturday, she remembered; they bought some jeans and sweatshirts and an anorak for Da. Then they came out of the shop and found themselves in the middle of a march, with banners and slogans and drums. Ma whispered to her that it was the anniversary of a hunger-striker who had died in prison the year before, and the people were mourning.

But Noreen looked at them, and knew they weren't mourning. Most of them weren't anyway; or maybe they did once. But what she saw now was their eyes, and those were hard, just like those of the Orangemen.

They were afraid, she and Ma. She could tell Ma was

afraid because she walked so fast and because of the way her mouth was. They were on the wrong side, and everyone must know; people must be able to see just by looking at them, see their guilt – only they didn't even know why they were guilty (just like Jesus saying, you have all crucified me; it is your fault, because everyone's . . . It was incomprehensible, and frightening).

Ma grabbed Noreen's hand, and they scuttled through the black-lined ranks of white, hard faces that were torn with silent bitterness. They got away all right.

The Twelfth was different, though: it was all noise – singing and flutes and gaily waving flags carrying King Billy and the words 'Lest we forget'. Noreen ran with all the others, skipping girls and kids, oblivious to their mothers' railing, to catch up with the parade in the large field set aside for the occasion. Here proud girls joined their uniformed lads, mothers found children and relatives (never husbands). There were hamburgers, hotdogs, fizzy drinks and ice-cream. Some people had brought picnics, which they spread out on the grass, frantically warding off wasps and dogs and other people's children. Couples lay down beneath the trees, drinking beer, and uniforms were gradually discarded. It was a time for drinking and lazing, being full with alcohol and singing.

Noreen found Kenny down by the road, ripping the top off a bottle of Wee Willie, using the door handle of the telephone kiosk. He put his mouth underneath to catch the foaming liquid as it oozed out. He offered some to Noreen, and she gasped as she gulped it down. He laughed at her.

'Come on, then!' 'Girl', he called her. His arm went round her so easily, and they joined the rest of the boys, a group of about eight, of whom she recognized two: the ginger-haired fellow who had been in the car that first Sunday, and the tall, older one, with glasses and a moustache, called PJ. Beside him sat a large, pink-faced girl who stared at Noreen. She hardly noticed though, as she sat there in the long grass with them, sharing their beer bottles, the sun warm on her neck, and Kenny's hand laying claim to her. She could sense that he was proud of her.

They sat watching all the people going by, and sang 'The Sash' and other songs which Noreen had never heard before. She thought it must be the best day of her life. It was such a wonderful, lazy time, with the sun beating down on them, the warm, releasing alcohol, his kisses in the grass. He didn't care about the others laughing, and nor did she, as he pressed her into the grass beneath slow white clouds.

When she sat up again, she could see her parents in the distance, Da with his belly looking comfortable in the lightweight trousers, and Ma in a short-sleeved dress with flowers on. She was licking an ice-cream.

'I'll have to go.' Noreen stood up, shaking herself from Kenny's grasp.

He looked peeved. 'You'll come to the dance with me, though,' he asked, 'next Friday?'

'I don't know. Maybe.' She was already running in the opposite direction.

'We'll pick you up,' he called after her. 'Eight o'clock?' She didn't reply.

'And where did you get to?' asked Ma.

'Just a fellow I met.' She blushed.

'Looked like a rough lot to me,' Da remarked.

'Oh, sure isn't it the Twelfth?' said Ma. 'Sure everybody's happy . . .'

They started making their way back to the car. Beneath a big tree, Noreen could see a group of fellows throwing their bottles in the air and singing 'The Sash'. She could just hear the words, over and over again: 'It is old but it is beautiful . . .' It was a song that filled her with warmth.

She felt sick with nerves that Friday night. She wore her black jeans and a blouse with yellow spots on it, the only clean one she had left.

She was fifteen now, after all. Da had agreed, after a hushed consultation with Ma, that she might go out with the 'young fellow', so long as she was in by eleven o'clock. She was of an age . . . She heard their muffled voices in the sitting-room. He liked the idea that Kenny played in the band, at least. That must say something for him.

Ma wanted to know all about it, of course. 'Where will yous go? What'll you wear? I hope yous won't be drinking.'

Later, when Da was working on his papers at his bureau in the good room, Ma looked up from her knitting and cleared her throat in that way she had, when she was about to say something important.

'Noreen – you will always be careful, won't you?'

'Careful? How d'you mean?'

Ma cleared her throat again. 'I mean – with men, like.' She looked down at her knitting pattern.

Noreen felt herself blushing. 'Oh. Of course.'

'You know –' Ma spoke quietly, her eyes on the door of the room next door, 'some men will tell you any sweet nothing to get what they want – and then they'll drop you like a hot brick.' Her needles started clicking again.

Noreen shifted in her seat. She didn't enjoy these talks with Ma. They filled her with embarrassment and with a vague guilt, a feeling that somehow she was dirty, inherently dirty, and she had to stop Ma from seeing.

It was the same sort of feeling that she had had when she was wee and had wet her pants during the prayers at the end of school. She could feel it coming on as she closed her eyes and clasped her hands together, murmuring along with the others, 'Our Father, who art in Heaven'. As she got to 'Hallowed be Thy name', she was aware of the wetness beginning to trickle irrepressibly down her legs, forming a large puddle on the floor beside her desk. She clenched her legs together, but it kept on coming out, and there was nothing she could do about it. Afterwards she stood waiting until all the other children left the room. Luckily her place was at the end of a row, at the back of the classroom.

The teacher saw her standing there. 'All right, Noreen?' he asked.

She nodded, pretending to look for something in her desk. The teacher gathered his books together and went. Noreen sneaked out quickly, leaving the awful tell-tale puddle behind her. It was the same sort of feeling now with Ma, as if she were trying to stop Ma from seeing the wicked part of her which sometimes seeped out quite unbidden; as if she didn't want Ma to see what she was really like inside – her secret thoughts and feelings, which were half-hidden even from herself.

Before Noreen had gone on to grammar school, Ma had sat her down one day and told her about the birds and the bees and the blood – all that, in a blushing, roundabout sort of way. And as she grew up, she learned all about how you must save yourself for marriage, or no fellow would touch you with a barge-pole. And sure wasn't that what everyone wanted, in the end? A boyfriend, some nice fellow to come along one day and marry you. What else was there, after all? You worked at some job or other for a year or two after you left school, just to fill in the time: then you met a fellow and got married. Then there were the children (and maybe love, too? You dared hope . . .)

But in school, Noreen smoked guiltily with the other girls in the loos and learned about the so-called liberating Pill; and she learned about other things too – sinful things, which Ma would have been shocked at. For a schoolfriend once lent her a certain book, which she kept hidden in a safe place beneath her bed and read avidly each night.

'You're burning the midnight oil,' Da remarked casually.

She nodded, horrified. But Da just smiled and went on perusing his paper. She had to go on reading, even though there were expressions which she didn't properly understand; she had to read more, to know . . .

Then Ma discovered the shameful, dog-eared epic when she was cleaning the room one day, and she held it, trembling, before Noreen when she came in from school that afternoon. After the confrontation it went straight into the bin, and no more was said about it; but Noreen felt that Ma looked at her differently after that. There had been other such books in the past, and later the same schoolfriend offered a book about an abortionist; but Noreen, torn between fascination and horror, declined. It was for her a glimpse into a forbidden, disturbingly free world of which she had previously known nothing and in which, in reality, she found hard to believe. She found it hard to believe in this Pill, and in the free and easy encounters that were described in the books. The one she liked best was a tale of passion, rape and violence; the auburn-haired heroine loved virginally, was raped, fought, and loved again. This book, with its saga of stolen passion and defilement, was easier for Noreen to believe in. For there was no place here for any Pill – here, where Thomas next door drove his tractor, red-faced from sun and girls, where you got engaged years before you ever married, and then it was a white wedding. Everyone came round to see the presents, which you'd lay out on your bed with the name tags alongside, so that they could all see who had given what. They'd smile and look forward to your wedding day and to your new house and baby. You'd give them tea and scones and sandwiches and be glad of their presents and of their departure. No room here for any Pill.

Ma's needles clicked on relentlessly. Noreen glanced up at her. She was sitting in her old armchair by the table lamp, which was lit now, as the evening was growing in the room. The light made the shadows under her eyes more harsh than usual, and it caught the grey streaks in her brown hair. Her legs were crossed at the ankles; she wore her old mules, and you could see the varicose veins running up her legs beneath her stockings.

Ma looked up and caught Noreen's eye. 'But, Noreen –' She hesitated, watching the door of the good room. 'If anything ever happened – well, we'd stand by you, you know?'

'Yes, Ma, thanks.' Noreen got up and went out quickly, because she couldn't bear to see Ma sitting there in the darkening room, getting older and saying these things.

She was ready far too early: by seven, and she sat there all dressed up, waiting, not sure when they would come, or even if they would come. Eight o'clock came and went. At five past they arrived in the familiar white car; she saw it pull up on the other side of the hedge, and she leapt up as they hooted the horn.

'I should let them wait a bit,' advised Ma.

'Anyone wi' any decency would knock,' grumbled Da. He was pulling on his shirt by the fire, getting ready to go out to the Lodge.

'Don't you be late, now,' Ma called from the kitchen. 'Or there won't be any other times!'

She didn't know how she would tell them that she had to be in by eleven. They'd laugh. For a minute she almost wished she were staying in. She heard the horn again.

'Go on, then!' scolded Ma.

The front door slammed behind her. She got in the back.

'Hiya, Noreen.' PJ was driving, and the plump girl, Louise, was beside him. She said nothing. You could smell her perfume. Kenny was all dressed up in his suit and tie for getting into the dance, and he loved her in the back, with his kisses and touch. She was lost in his coarse feel and the smells of smoke and alcohol and maleness (maleness – what was it, she wondered. The aftershave, the clothes, the cigarettes . . .), the radio blaring as they sped along. Once she looked up and caught PJ's eyes on them in the mirror.

It was only a short drive to Robinson's Bar.

'Someone will shout "Police!" ' Kenny reassured her, as they walked over from the car. 'There's no problem. And PJ here has friends . . .'

Yet doing things that were wrong no longer worried her as they once would have done. She no longer felt the same guilt; as if, with that first dance, she had crashed some barrier, overstepped some boundary, so that now there were no limits.

They squeezed in round a table between glasses and elbows. It made you dizzy coming in from outside – the people crowded together beneath the bright lights, drinking and shouting. It took so long to reach the bar, that they bought several rounds in one go. Noreen drank vodka, for she didn't know what else to ask for. She knocked it back like the others did, feeling it sear all the way down to her tummy. It made her feel warm and happy and lovely, and that this was all she ever wanted. The best days of her life, surely. She looked benignly upon everything as from a great distance. She could feel herself smiling a silly smile, but it didn't matter. She was so happy.

The fellows round the table were telling loud stories and laughing, leaning forward over their glasses. There was a bit of fighting over in the far corner, but Noreen felt as if it were all very distant somehow. She liked the vodka, and she drank the other two glasses which they'd bought for her, only vaguely aware of Kenny's hand on her leg. PJ looked at her from across the table. Louise was toying with her glass, swilling the vodka round and round. She caught Noreen's eye once, and Noreen half-smiled, but the plump girl only stared at her.

The first and only other time she had ever been in a pub was that time when she was staying at Eileen McAllister's house, after Granny had died, and Eileen's cousins had arrived unexpectedly from Warrenpoint. Eileen and Noreen were sent down to fetch Mr McAllister from the pub, where he served sometimes, sloshing the glasses and wisecracking.

Noreen hadn't ever been in a place like that before, what with her Da being good-living. It filled her with strangeness – the stale smell of beer coming out at you into the sunshine with the swift babble of men's talk, and inside the morning sun streaking and stippling the heavy curtains through the smoke; the round, polished tables crowded with men. That was the 'Public Bar', a close wee room where all the men yelled and drank. There were pictures on the wall: one was supposed to be the men of the 1916 Easter Rising, defending the General Post Office in Dublin, but Noreen didn't know what that was; and another of an old man in a cap, brandishing a tall glass of beer and a gun at the camera. It gave her the creeps, that one.

Eileen's Da gave them some crisps, and another man with a plump, pink face winked at them from behind the bar. Mr McAllister said that he would come soon, soon, and sent them packing back home, where Mrs McAllister gave them weak tea and cheesecake out of a packet – two helpings each. Noreen was like family, then. But that was before – a long time before – the big dance.

Noreen stood up and somehow managed to make her way through all the tables and people to the loos at the far end of the bar. Her former good mood seemed to have vanished and she felt inexplicably depressed. Inside the loos, there was a girl asleep on the floor, and another vomiting into the stained basin just above her. Noreen came out again quickly.

She caught sight of the clock on the wall. Twenty to ten. She hadn't told them about being home by eleven, she remembered dully. They would be heading for the dance next. She would never be home in time.

They were all standing up to go when she got back to the table, and Kenny led her out by the arm, not too steady himself. They got into the car and began driving off, but Noreen immediately started to feel sick, and they had to stop again while she staggered out and was sick by a lamp-post. She was only dimly aware of Louise swearing, and some woman coming out of the house they were stopped by to tell them off.

'Shame on yous!' Noreen could hear her saying. 'Yous should know better – thon poor wee girl. Take her home, for God's sake. No, wait, I'll get her some tea.'

A minute later she was back with the tea, which Noreen sipped, but it was too sweet, and she spat it out again. The women tut-tutted crossly. 'It's for your own good, you know. What would your parents say, if they knew? Oh, Lord – take her home, yous lads.'

Then somehow she was back in the car and they were

driving on again. She could tell from their raised voices that they were all talking about her, but she couldn't make sense of what they were saying. They arrived at the dance-hall, which was a blur of lights, and Kenny and Louise got out.

Kenny's face was looming in at her. It wouldn't keep still. 'PJ'll take you home,' she heard him say. 'I'll see you again – sure you've had too much. You look after her now, you shite!'

'Like she was my own sister.'

They were gone. Everything seemed beyond her control, and she was content to lean her head back against the seat, close her eyes. PJ swung the car round in the car-park, and then they were spinning back the way they had come. He drove fast, with the radio on. All Noreen could see was the road rushing at them out of the dark, like a dream.

'You're not afeared, are you, Noreen?' he asked her once, trying to see her face in the mirror.

She turned her head from side to side, the only bit of herself that she could move. Everything was such an effort. 'No.' She felt powerless. The whole thing had an air of unreality about it, the helplessness of a nightmare.

They were slowing down. The car stopped. He flicked off the headlights. Noreen peered out. They were in a lay-by on the Dromara Road.

She felt more sober all of a sudden. 'What're you doing?'

He was out and opening her door. A car flashed by, lighting him up momentarily, then it was gone. PJ was in the back beside her already, and his arm creeping round her. She pulled away. 'Please, don't.'

'Noreen! Sure you can't see anything in him – Kenny. Ach, he's only a wee boy, for God's sake. Have a bit of sense. You need someone mature, love . . . And sure Kenny would never know. We needn't tell him.'

Oh, God. It was the last thing she wanted. With Kenny, at least she felt safe.

But PJ was kissing her, and his mouth was so big, it seemed to gobble up her face. His moustache got inside her mouth like some insidious, hairy insect. She pushed at him, and she could see his glasses all steamed up like the windows of the car. She thought she might be sick again. PJ was tall and strong and bony, and he tried to make her do what was labelled in her mind 'the awful thing'.

She didn't want any man, ever, to do that to her.

Oh, please, please . . .

He kept reaching for her hand and placing it on his trousers, then inside, so that she was forced to feel some hard, pulsating thing of which she had never dreamt. Well, that wasn't quite true. Something had happened once, though she'd always tried to tell herself no, it hadn't.

It was when she was wee – eight, maybe – and walking home from school. Eileen turned off into the estate and she was left to walk the last bit alone, down the main road, then sharp turn down the lane home. She used to pant along here after Ma sometimes.

But this day there was no one, and the red van, like a post van, pulled up beside her just before she turned off the main road. The man in it (a bit plump, with untidy hair, mouse brown) asked her the way to some place,

70

Bradford's Farm, which she'd never heard of. It was strange, for you tended to know all the people round your way; the man must be hopelessly lost.

'I don't know it.' She shook her head, and made to walk on.

Then he started laughing.

'Look here!' he said, pointing to something inside the van.

She looked. And there it was. Horrible. She swore at him, the worst word she knew, and then she ran all the way home and hid in her bedroom until teatime. She felt dirty – as if somehow it was she who had done something. She lay on the bed and wept with disgust and rage. She never told anyone about the awful thing.

PJ gave up with a sigh and drove her home.

'You're a nice girl, Noreen,' he said, before she ran from the car. 'A very nice girl.'

She didn't know what he meant.

She got into the house quickly. Ma was sitting in her dressing-gown, watching the news, sipping at a cup of tea.

'Nice time?' she inquired.

Noreen glanced at the clock. Quarter to eleven. 'Oh, yes,' she said, 'lovely.'

'And how was the dance?'

'Oh, it was good.'

Ma was looking at her. She pretended to yawn. 'Think I'll go to bed now, I'm done.'

'Are you all right?'

'Of course I'm all right!'

She sidled off, praying that Ma couldn't smell the drink.

'Well, you can tell me all about it in the morning. Won't you?'

'If you want. Goodnight.'

'Goodnight, love.'

She dropped her clumsy body into bed and slept until she heard the gates swing open for Da in the early hours. Then she struggled for consciousness, but it seemed as though she were being physically pressed down, down, by the heavy night in the room, and she succumbed to the dark waves until the unpleasant morning.

Ma said that if going out made Noreen ill, then she had better stay at home in future. She felt Noreen's forehead and made her spend the day in bed. Over-excitement, maybe . . . Noreen was conscious of Ma's eyes resting on her a moment longer. She was careful not to let it happen again; she stuck at two or three vodkas and kept away from PJ, who was just as calm and cool behind his glasses the next time he saw her as if nothing had happened. She put it from her mind.

They relied on him for getting about: mostly to the bar, sometimes the Friday dance, now and then a Sunday afternoon in Newcastle. They even spent one Saturday morning watching him play golf. Louise bit her nails and looked bored; Kenny cheered at vital moments, and PJ swore at him. Afterwards they had lunch in some hotel by the sea – PJ treated them. Kenny nudged Noreen and told her to eat all she could. They had veal, which Noreen had never tasted before, and 'sauté' potatoes, followed by a raspberry meringue pudding. Kenny thought it was great and finished up all the chocolate mints that came on a wee saucer with the coffee.

'We're living now,' he said to Noreen. 'Jesus, we're living now.'

Noreen poked at the demerara sugar, which came in a cut glass bowl with a silver spoon: amazing stuff which cascaded softly like a pile of exquisite crystals. But she didn't like the strong coffee any more than she liked the cutlets of veal – soft, squidgy stuff which made you think of poor blubbery calves cooped up like soft fungi in the dark. She went to the loo instead, a long, carpeted room with polished mirrors and clean hand towels and a bowl of pot-pourri between the two basins. The toilet was made of dark wood, and she spent a long time sitting on it. The paper was soft, the flushing discreet, and then she found, to her consternation, that she could not open the door again. She banged, but no one heard through the beautiful, papered walls. It was Louise who eventually found her, having come to reapply her make-up.

'Get me out!' said Noreen. 'Please, Louise.'

There was a pause. 'What's it worth to you, then?'

'Come on! Just get me out.'

'I don't see why I should.'

She could hear Louise's cosmetic bag clicking open and shut, followed by a silence, during which she must be puffing on her powder. Then the raking of a comb through her curly hair. Footsteps – and the door swung shut.

But a short while later there was a scuffling at the window above her. The hotel boy jumped down inside, very nimble, very polite, and with only the hint of a smirk on his face. After a few minutes' struggling, he slid back the bolt and let her out.

She met Louise's eyes across the table. This time the plump girl didn't look away, as she often did. She stared at Noreen coolly, with no more than a hint of malice in her wide, innocent eyes, but Noreen didn't miss the challenge in them.

The summer was nearly over now. Eileen must be long back from her holidays, but she never called, and Noreen heard from Geraldine, whom she met in Isabel's shop one day, that Eileen was going with that fellow Brendan. Geraldine said it with a strange air of satisfaction, and Noreen hurried out with her loaf of Veda. She was half-way home when she remembered that she still owed Geraldine for the dance that night.

Kenny got a job as a machine operator in the science lab in Queen's and soon he managed to buy a car of his own: a second-hand red Toledo, in which he taught Noreen to drive around the country roads.

He told Noreen that she was a cracker, and he took her to the dances, to the pictures, and to the amusements by the sea, where the young couples sat in their cars along the front on Sunday nights. They all watched each other walking up and down, or kissing, or racing the cars up and down the main street, and ate hamburgers.

He never liked coming into the house when he called, though Ma always asked him, but now and then he did, and it was strange to see him balanced on the edge of one of the good armchairs in his checked trousers and yellow V-necked sweater, knees well apart, the hair on his face. ('You should make him shave,' Ma told Noreen in the safety of the kitchen.) He and Da would mumble a few polite evening words to each other, and Da told him to be sure and look after Noreen. Kenny nodded, in a mystified sort of way, and leapt up as soon as Noreen appeared with her jacket and bag. Da shook his hand before he finally got out the door. They were both relieved when it was over.

Kenny never took Noreen to his house, for he said his parents might get the wrong idea about her, going to grammar school, and her Ma working in the barracks – that sort of thing. Sure there was no need, anyhow. Noreen was relieved, for she could think of nothing worse.

Kenny was tender and loving, and he belonged to a secret organization. Soon after they started going together, he confided in Noreen that he had a uniform which he had to put in the wash bit by bit, in case his Ma got wise to it. When Noreen asked him what he did exactly, he became very serious and a bit embarrassed, muttering about 'watching people'. It wasn't pleasant, of course, but someone had to do it, didn't they? You had to do your bit. He made Noreen promise never, never to let on to anyone else what he had just told her, or else his life might be in danger. Noreen nodded, solemn.

'Whatever happened to your Fenian friend?' he asked her once.

'Oh, we've lost touch,' Noreen answered vaguely.

'Good thing too,' said Kenny, shaking out a cigarette. 'Good thing.'

But Noreen couldn't forget Eileen so easily, and she

wondered if Eileen ever thought about her. Sunday afternoons seemed strange, now that they no longer walked the roads together. Arm in arm they used to go, planning their futures as they went: how they'd leave school, find jobs, and go out to spend their money in the evenings. Then, after a bit, they'd meet two nice boys and get married, have children, and live near each other. They would wheel the babies out in the prams, sit in the park with them in the sun, and talk and plan and reminisce, like they did now. It was good, remembering things you'd done together, and thinking what you might do. And of course, their husbands would get along famously; they'd all go down the pub together on Friday nights, and their parents could babysit. Oh, it would be grand!

Eileen always stopped in front of the prams to talk to the babies, which opened gummy mouths at her, like wee old men. Noreen would walk on, impatient, wanting to get away from the frills and the smell of milky sick. Eileen seemed to take naturally to all that, somehow; well, girls did, didn't they? Noreen wondered about herself sometimes.

Eileen wanted a white wedding too. A big, frilly white wedding, with hundreds of people – all the ones she'd ever known. Her niece could be the flower girl; she'd blonde hair and big blue eyes – the most lovely wee thing, only three. And then there would be a romantic honeymoon somewhere, maybe Italy or Switzerland. It would be the only chance she'd ever get. But they wouldn't be able to afford it, of course; other things were much more important, like a fridge and a washing machine. She wouldn't really mind, though.

Oh, yes, she'd be a virgin when she married – otherwise she couldn't have a proper white wedding. But her husband would probably be experienced, or he wouldn't know what to do in bed. They'd both giggled, then.

Noreen wasn't at all sure about white weddings. She wouldn't want to go tripping up the aisle with a great long veil flowing after her, and all those people watching. Eileen had suggested that they could have a joint wedding, and then they'd be in it together. That would be fun. There'd likely be a problem, though, with the churches; she wasn't sure about that. Maybe one of them should change religion! Noreen said that she didn't care what she was. What difference did it make, after all, what you were? Most people didn't give a damn – they were just people wanting to get on with their lives. Sure weren't there the groceries to buy, the house to clean, the brew to draw; the kids to get through school in the hope that somehow they might get decent jobs. Life to be lived . . . Noreen and Eileen nodded together, wise wee women.

All that had mattered in those days was that they two were friends. But now Noreen had lost her best friend, Eileen McAllister. It was not meant to be an abandonment; it was just that she, Noreen, had gone on to places where Eileen could not follow: into the Loyalist strongholds where 'Fenian' was a profanity.

Now Noreen sat in Robinson's Bar, squashed between Kenny and his mates, who sang 'The Sash' when they got full. Noreen sang it too. All that stuff about ancestors and battles and victories made you feel fervent and warm and close; you shared something. You were caught up in the greatness of loyalty to a cause and determination to survive, to stand firm against all threats to the Protestant way of life (which was surely yours). Your heart sang to the familiar rousing tunes of triumph that recalled King Billy's victories over the Catholics . . . Only now and then did you wonder who they were, these Catholics, this other side, which you feared and hated.

You got the same answers. Always the same answers.

The Catholics: troublemakers, murderers, who've had it in for the Protestants all along and tried to force us out of the country. Sure that's why we all support King Billy, the great William of Orange, the one who, in the famous Battle of the Boyne, saved us from the Papists.

But who exactly are these Papists?

They're the ones who put us under siege at Derry and committed God only knows how many other atrocities against us, hidden from history. Hidden they may be, but not forgotten. Long live King Billy!

They're the ones who killed Geordie McFarlane in that bomb down Church Street; the ones who shot the two brothers in the Plough last Tuesday; ach, they're all the same. Anyhow, if you're so worried about them, why don't you go and bloody well join them? You don't know what you're talking about; it's never happened to you. Fine words get us nowhere. You and your grammar school – think you're too good for us, don't you? Only snobs have education; you're different from us, think you're better. Well, we all know about your Fenian friend. They're all the same, don't you see? They stand for the same thing. Just you keep your mouth shut and you'll be OK, though. You're a harmless enough wee girl most of the time. And you do sing 'The Sash'.

The point is, we mustn't ever let them get away with it, see. We must defend ourselves and our way of life. The dead mustn't go unavenged! We mustn't ever forget.

'We must never forget,' said Kenny. 'Never. We must avenge our dead, see – for there's no bloody God to do it.'

5

School had started again, and Eileen looked the other way on the bus. Then she took to catching the later one.

Some Sunday afternoons Kenny worked on his car, and there was nothing to do, nothing. Da sat there by the window with his Bible, and Ma wrote her letters. Noreen flicked through a book and felt as if her head might burst.

Ma put down her pen and sighed. 'Whatever happened to Eileen McAllister?' she asked.

'Eileen? We fell out.'

Da was quiet by the window. She could sense him listening.

'Oh, life is too short, Noreen!' said Ma. 'Anyhow – that's your business. But couldn't you do something? Quit moping like a sick hen and give my head peace.'

She picked up the pen again and tapped it thoughtfully against her teeth, then began writing.

Noreen slammed out and took off down the lane. There were no tractors today, no one working the fields – just the odd car. Everything seemed quiet, resting, for it was Sunday. People were dozing after their Sunday dinner. Only the Jack Russell next door rushed down the garden and yapped at Noreen's legs. She felt like giving it a good kick, but she could sense Mrs Baird watching her from behind the venetian blind.

She went round in a big circle, past Malcolm's house, then up by the school and along the main road where the new houses were being built: a group of ten 'luxury bungalows' beside the council estate where Eileen lived. The whole area was being developed now; more and more people were getting out from Lisburn, and you no longer knew all the faces. The farmers sold off a plot of land here and there to make their money – even Thomas.

When the Logans had first moved out, it was just country, apart from the council estate along the road. There were no strange gangs of kids on bikes then, no unknown cars driving past. It was that summer, when Noreen was new, that she first got to know Eileen McAllister. Da had been promoted to manager that year, and soon afterwards they decided to make the move out to a bigger place in the country, just like Ma had always wanted (she was a country girl, really). It was a low, white-washed cottage with a slate roof covering the old thatch, and roses in the garden. There were a couple of outhouses and even a bit of land out the back, where a stream ran through between boulders and flowering gorse.

Noreen, a bit lonely at first in the new place, made a gorse house down there. She discovered that you could burrow through between the bushes, along wee paths made by rabbits, until you came to a hollow amongst the prickly flowers which smelled of coconut. She sat there listening to the stream, which spilled and pattered over the rocks, and she even saw a kingfisher flash by, a dart of blue. Three times she saw it altogether. The gorse house was Noreen's secret place, and no one knew about it, not even Ma.

Other times she would walk out across the fields in the evening, over the slowly rotting bridge above the stream, up the boggy hill and through the fence on to the main road. The sweet van came to the estate at seven o'clock each evening; well, it wasn't just a sweet van, it sold other things too – fish and chips, tinned things – but Noreen was only interested in the sweets. She bought packs of XLs. Da didn't like her buying chewing-gum – he thought it was a dirty habit, but it was her pocket money, and they'd said she could use it to buy whatever she wanted. She wanted chewing-gum. You got four bits to a pack, a blue, a green, a yellow and a red. Noreen liked the red ones best.

There was a queue at the van every evening. Lots of people went there, especially the housewives, to buy tins of things, and the older kids, who bought fish and chips and then went off together, laughing and talking. No one spoke to Noreen, apart from the man selling the stuff, who said, 'Yes, love?', and she spoke to no one, for she was too shy. But a ginger-haired girl stared at her each evening as she went past Noreen with a load of stuff in her arms; up into the estate she went, and Noreen could see her turn into one of the houses up there. On the third evening the girl was right in front of her in the queue. She just bought some sweets this time – some liquorice and two lollipops – and then she sat down on the wall, swinging her legs, until Noreen came away with her XLs.

'You're new, aren't you?' she said then.

Noreen stopped beside her and nodded unwillingly,

clutching the chewing-gum in her hand, which was suddenly sweaty. She didn't like admitting that she was new. It put her at a disadvantage. She wondered whether to walk on. She looked at the girl, who had on a flowered dress which was too short and grubby knee socks. She was sucking on the first lollipop, which was one of those that changes colour as you suck.

'You live in the old cottage down there, don't you?'

Noreen nodded again.

'What's your name, then?'

'Noreen.'

'Noreen. Oh, Noreen.' She tried it out slowly, emphasizing the *Nor*.

'What's yours?'

The girl considered her for a moment. 'Eileen,' she said then. 'McAllister,' she added after a pause, as if this had some significance.

Noreen made to move on, but the girl, Eileen, stopped her with a hand on her arm. Noreen saw that she wore a silver cross round her neck. 'Why don't you come with us, then?' asked Eileen. 'Down the fields. I can show you places . . .'

'Oh, I don't know . . .' Noreen shook her head. Ma and Da would wonder where she was, and she felt reluctant to go with the girl, whom she didn't know, and who wore a cross round her neck.

'Are you stuck-up then, or what?'

'Oh, it's not that.' Noreen hesitated. She shouldn't go, she knew. Ma and Da liked her in by nine. And the girl looked – well, she had the feeling they would disapprove. Still, she didn't want to be thought stuck-up. It was a sort of a test, she knew. She had to go.

So she followed Eileen away down the fields behind the council houses, away across the builders' land, which was full of dunes and pits, embryos of new houses and skeletons of old. They played uneasy hide-and-seek up and down decaying stairs, crept across exposed rafters, and messed about in the earth dunes and valleys left to waste by the builders. Noreen began to enjoy herself. Eileen took her through the bit of woodland where the older ones went snogging in the late summer evenings – what you could see then! They both giggled. They followed wee paths where the branches sometimes came so low, you had to crawl under them. Then you came suddenly to a river which ran wide and fast. On each side there were steep banks which no one could ever climb up. In one place there was a black pipe which came out of the grass and ran high above the river. It took the water to the houses. They stood looking across to the other side.

'Dare you to cross it,' Eileen said then. 'You're a coward if you don't.'

The evening was still. You could hear a cow bellow, and the far-off hypnotic drone of a tractor. Noreen felt her face hot. She looked down into the water, and it was silent, so that you knew it was deep, very deep. You might fall down there, and no one would ever hear you. You'd become silence. She looked up again. She saw a scrap of washing waving in the wind up by the council houses.

'All right, then,' she said. She had to, or Eileen would think she was a coward.

Eileen was quiet as Noreen sat down on the bit of pipe that lay in the grass. Gradually she inched forward, until her legs dangled above the water. The pipe was cold on the bare skin under her dress. She looked round. 'You have to come after me, though.'

'Oh aye,' said Eileen. 'After you.'

Noreen shuffled on without looking back again. She went over a raised bit that pinched her bare legs, then on, slowly, towards the middle. She could hear the river down there, but she kept her eyes on the other side. She was almost halfway, and then she looked down. There was the water far – oh, far – below, and, as she looked, she saw that it didn't just flow, but it swirled and puckered and sucked. She saw a red and white Coca-Cola can being swept along down there, and then came a battered Sunshine Squeeze. She sat very still for a whole minute, clinging to the metal with sweaty hands. Yet nothing could happen to her, could it, God? Please . . .

There was a shout from across the river. 'Go on, then! What're you waiting for?'

The nausea passed. She forced herself on, painfully. She was almost there. Almost touching the other side. Careful. Firm ground. Her head rushed as she felt the grass on the other side. She collapsed in it, hardly noticing that Eileen was beginning the slow crossing.

Eileen was resolute. She never stopped in the middle, but crept on, inch by inch, keeping up a low monologue all the time. Noreen could see her lips moving.

'Oh, sweet Jesus!' She threw herself down in the grass beside Noreen, and lay there with her eyes closed for a bit. Her chest was heaving beneath her cardigan, but it gradually slowed down until it seemed as if she must be asleep. Her pale face was pink with exertion. Suddenly she opened her eyes and looked up at Noreen. Her eyes were very green, with tiny brown flecks in them, and a bit mad-looking somehow. It was only now that Noreen realized what was a bit odd about them: Eileen's left eye was turned in ever so slightly, just enough to give the bizarre impression that not only was she looking at Noreen but at someone else at the same time.

'What're you staring at?' she asked now.

Noreen looked away, confused. She could hardly explain that she was as fascinated by Eileen's flawed eye as by the silver cross around her white neck. It was a defect which, partly because of Eileen's defensiveness over it, acted to mellow her boldness and make her a strangely poignant figure. Somehow it drew Noreen to her even more.

'I never thought you'd do it,' she said then. She sat up, shaking her head so that wisps of grass fell from her hair. 'To look at you, I never thought you would.'

They walked back to the houses together, sharing chewing-gum and liquorice, and Noreen glowed with Eileen's careless praise. It didn't seem to matter about the scolding she got when she arrived home. Da told her off for being thoughtless, quite thoughtless; but Ma soon relented and said, 'Bring the wee girl home, Noreen.' For she'd told them about Eileen.

And so it was that the next day Eileen came all the way to Noreen's house, and Ma gave them squash and biscuits. She asked Eileen all sorts of questions, like where did she live, exactly? And where did she go to school? Ma's face flickered slightly. She paused. What did her daddy do? she asked then. And what was her mammy's name? It turned out that she'd come across Mary McAllister already in the shop. You couldn't help knowing about people. A big woman – worked in the hospital part-time. Oh yes, Ma had seen her. She smiled.

Afterwards they wandered through the rooms together, and Eileen kept picking things up and putting them down again.

'It's great,' she said once. 'I wish we'd a house like this.'

And Noreen had felt guilty because Eileen had to live on the estate in the council house with all her brothers and sisters and the drunks and the old cars.

Later she showed Eileen the secret gorse house down the fields. No one else knew about it; it was a secret now between her and Eileen. They shuffled around the garden together in the big cardboard box that had brought Ma's new washing machine, then ran about knee-deep in the wild grass out the back, where the tang of mint swept you and frogs leapt unexpectedly.

Eileen's garden was only a wee square, and even that was all taken up with her Ma's washing and her Da's old cars beneath, rusting bits which he tinkered with at weekends. Her Ma grumbled about it and said they ought to have somewhere bigger, they could maybe afford it now, but her Da only said, sure you're never happy, yous women, and that was that.

The place was just the same now – kids playing in the road, and painted gates at the end of narrow concreted paths. It all seemed homely and familiar.

She swung open the gate of No. 6. The front box of garden was newly mown, and there was a motorbike glove lying on the path. The front door was slightly ajar. A smell of stew came from inside. Noreen rapped, lightly. No one came at first, and she was about to peer in through the window, when there was a noise behind her and there was Mrs McAllister on the step, undoing the last of her curlers.

'Oh, it's you, Noreen,' she said, through the pins in her mouth. She was clearly taken aback. 'Long time no see.'

'Aye.' Noreen tried not to look too hard at the curlers. They were pink, all apart from one, which was purple.

'Well.' Mrs McAllister seemed not to know quite what to say next. The curlers were all out now, and the hair sat in ridges, which Mrs McAllister began combing through. 'How's your mother, then? Keeping all right?'

'Aye.'

'Da all right? Still working himself into the ground?'

'Aye, I suppose so.' She hesitated. 'Would Eileen be in, Mrs McAllister?'

'Eileen?' repeated Mrs McAllister, as if she couldn't quite remember who Eileen was. 'Oh, yes. You'd better come in. I'll give her a shout. I do believe she's going out, though.'

Noreen squeezed past Mrs McAllister's stomach, which stuck out more than usual in a striped dress with buttons down the front.

Michael was sitting on the sofa, with his feet up on the coffee-table, reading the paper. He glanced at Noreen and carried on reading.

'Eileen! Eileen!' Mrs McAllister was calling from the foot of the stairs.

A faint 'What?'

'Noreen's here, Eileen!'

'What?'

'Noreen's here! Noreen Logan.' Mrs McAllister came back into the room, shaking her head. 'She'll be down in a minute, Noreen. Are you taking me to work, Michael?'

He grunted. Mrs McAllister looked at Noreen and raised her eyes to the ceiling. Noreen smiled sympathetically, grateful for the opportunity for a little collusion. Mrs McAllister started fussing again. 'Where's my bag? Have you seen my bag?' She was pulling at the cushions and opening cupboards. 'Have you seen it?'

Noreen didn't answer, because she didn't think Mrs McAllister was addressing her, and she hadn't seen it anyway. Michael got up and started jangling his keys.

'You were sitting on it all the time,' railed Mrs McAllister. 'You great lazy lump.'

Michael shrugged.

She retrieved the squashed tan handbag and found her lipstick. 'I have to be off now, Noreen.' She grimaced at herself in the mirror. 'But Eileen will be down in a minute.'

The door slammed. Noreen heard the van's engine revving up and accelerating off up the road, until it died away in the distance.

She looked around the room, which seemed to have changed little since that March, years ago, when Granny McCready died. They could have made her go and stay with Granny Logan, of course, but Noreen had cried and said she wouldn't, she wouldn't go! Granny with her ould stick and bulging veins and dark, fragile house. Ma had screamed, 'Oh, give my head peace! If there's any Christian love in the world, give my head peace!' Da had considered that gravely for a while and then conceded. She could stay with Eileen, 'under the circumstances'.

In Eileen's house there were holy pictures hanging on the walls of the sitting-room, which was decorated with white and gold striped wallpaper. 'Our Lady of Perpetual Succour' said one, and there was another of suffering Jesus on the cross. Noreen had never seen anything like it. Jesus had sad blue eyes and long hair and a beard; there was a white cloth round the tops of his legs, and you could see his heart, all bloody and in flames. Then there was a yapping cocker spaniel to contend with, and Eileen's Da, a big rough man with a jaw, who came in from the pub and sat watching the TV, quite oblivious to Jesus with his bleeding heart.

The McAllisters had a record player and an airing cupboard above the fire. Placed in a recess was a white statue: a figurine of a woman with long hair and a long dress and a halo thing on her head. Noreen was intrigued and took her down when no one was looking, but then Mrs McAllister came in from the tiny kitchen and snatched the object back from her with a sort of gasp.

'You must pray to Our Lady, child, not play with her!' She placed the figurine carefully back in the recess and made the sign of a cross on her chest. Noreen was appalled at what she had done, though she wasn't quite sure what it was; but she feared Mrs McAllister, who read the tea leaves and could tell your future from the cards. You had to be careful not to leave your cup lying around, or she'd find out things about you.

Noreen swung round. Eileen had come down the stairs so quietly that she hadn't heard her. They looked at each other. Eileen had on red corduroy jeans and a sweater. It looked as if she'd lost a bit of weight. But there was something else different too.

'Your eye!' said Noreen. 'You've had your eye done.'

Mind you, it had only been turned in ever such a little – you'd hardly have noticed – but Eileen had always been very conscious of it. She'd always wanted to go and get it done, but the thought of the operation frightened her.

'You never told me!' Noreen said now, reproachfully.

'Why should I?' asked Eileen.

Noreen dug her hands deeper into her jeans pockets. 'How was your holiday, then?'

'Holiday? Oh, OK, I suppose.' Her manner was cool. 'What brings you here, then?' It was hard to recall the closeness that lay behind them.

'I just wondered – if maybe you'd like to go for a walk or something . . . like we used to, you know . . .' Noreen shrugged. The whole thing seemed ridiculous all of a sudden. She wished she hadn't come.

Eileen stared at her. 'Oh, did you, now?' She looked away. 'Well, I can't,' she said abruptly. 'I'm going out.'

'Oh.' You could hear the clock ticking. 'Anyone nice?' She could guess, of course.

'Brendan, if you must know. You remember . . .?'

Oh, yes, she remembered.

A child was being hit next door. They could hear voices raised, crying. A bell started pinging on the cooker.

'I've to take Ma's stew out,' said Eileen, but she didn't move. Jesus looked down on them from the wall, his heart exposed, full of sorrow.

Eileen looked at her watch, pointedly. 'I'll have to be

going. Brendan's coming for me.' She was uneasy. She wanted Noreen out. 'You'd better go . . .'

Noreen knew. She started towards the door. It had been a mistake, all a mistake.

Eileen caught her arm. 'Look, Noreen – it doesn't matter, you know, what happened. Well, it did – but sure we can forget it now.'

'D'you mean that?'

'Yes, yes – let's forget it. I know you didn't really mean any harm . . .'

'Well – will we see each other sometimes, then?'

Eileen looked exasperated. 'Ach, Noreen – I'd like to, of course – but sure all that's over now. It couldn't be the same again.'

Noreen shook her head. 'I don't see – '

'We're not the same any more – we've different lives now, can't you see that?'

She couldn't see. Not really. She could still hear the bell pinging as the door closed behind her. She felt heavy as she went off down the path. The child that had been beaten was sitting snivelling on the next doorstep, but when she saw Noreen she stuck out her tongue. 'Prod bitch!'

Three more kids came rushing round the side of the house and immediately took up the chorus. 'Prod bitch, Prod bitch! Fuck off, fuck off!'

She felt sick. They were no more than eight years old. She noticed that there was IRA scrawled across the road. She didn't remember that there before. Then there was someone's spit running down her face, and hoots of laughter.

'You fuck off!' she yelled. 'Oh, you fuck off!' She walked away quickly.

'Away off home, you kids,' she could hear someone saying. 'Get away home.' It sounded like Eileen's voice.

She kept going and had made it to the end of the road before the tears started to fall.

The strangest thing happened. They were going to do her in. She sipped at her drink and felt the cold dragging down into her innards. She'd seen the fights and the scraps, of course, but she never thought it would happen to her.

Often it was some lads who'd had a bit too much to drink; their mates picked them up off the floor afterwards, and their girlfriends cried. But it was the girls' fights that frightened Noreen. She'd seen them in the loos at the bar, and outside the dance halls – how they scratched and tore and kicked and bit, and went for your face if they could. It was the relentlessness that got you, and a certain incongruity, for you had this idea that girls shouldn't fight.

You tried to avoid it by not getting involved with particular people, by not annoying them. You bowed and you scraped and you looked the other way when it was required of you, hoping they'd leave you alone.

But now they were out to get Noreen – blonde, plump Louise and her big sister, Patricia, who had lank, brown hair and wee piggy eyes squinting out of a fat face. Noreen shouldn't flirt with other people's boyfriends, see – and certainly not with PJ.

Kenny told her that once they kicked a girl to death in the loos of Robinson's Bar. They hadn't intended to kill her, so people said; just to teach her a lesson. She was a Fenian. But things had gone too far, somehow.

The police came to clear her up and ask questions, but no one was able to help them with their inquiries. No one had seen anything, no one knew anything. Everyone was afraid – not only of Louise and Patricia, but of their extensive family and circle of acquaintances who were always there in the background, protecting, threatening. It was the fear of the awful, nameless things which they might do that made people forget.

Besides, the girl was dead now. Nothing could be done to help her, and it hadn't really been intentional, after all. So people justified themselves. They didn't want trouble; they merely wanted to get on with their lives, and they had their families to think about, didn't they?

The next week Louise and Patricia were back in the bar, laughing and drinking, challenging with wide, innocent eyes anyone who dared stare. People shuddered and downed their drinks – and forgot. They would forget again.

Noreen would stay, of course, to see the thing out – whatever they might do. She had to. She sipped at her drink, but couldn't make it go down. The liquid stayed swilling in her mouth, warm and insipid, until at last she let it go.

'Come on,' said Kenny. 'We're going.'

She shook her head. But Kenny gripped her by the arm and his face was grim as he led her out. She could feel eyes on them from the bar, but no one bothered them. They got into the car without speaking. Kenny drove crazily, and he didn't break the awful silence until the car was stopped outside the cottage.

He thumped the wheel. 'How could you, how could you! Wi' PJ . . .'

'It's not true, you know.'

'How am I to know?' he demanded.

She felt tired; that he believed PJ rather than her.

'A right little bit,' said Kenny bitterly. 'That's what he said about you.'

She didn't want to hear it. She got out of the car, but he ran after her. 'All you care about is drinking and dancing!' He pinioned her against the wall of the house, with his desperation and screams and heaviness. 'You're no better than a whore!'

And there she was, still a virgin. Noreen didn't know whether to laugh or cry. She cried; Kenny could understand that. She cried into his jacket, which he brought close to her, and as she did so, it struck her that she no longer cared about him.

She let him take her back into the car. 'Maybe I was a bit harsh,' he whispered after a bit, repentant. 'But I can't bear to think you've been like that with other men.' Then he sobbed as if his heart would break, and she stroked his hair gently, shocked, for she had never seen a man cry before. He was so vulnerable, and yet she felt nothing for him, except perhaps a little pity.

As for virginity – she couldn't care less about that any more. Kenny's sobs became kisses which hurt, but she did not stop him. Better to discard her wretched virginity once and for all. She had some idea that by doing so she would cross some boundary and become properly a woman. Oh, to be ripe and strong and full and secret with knowledge! To blossom . . . It wouldn't matter about marriage, nor about what people thought. She didn't care about those things. The important thing was that she would be herself, Noreen Logan, a woman travelling through life, and she would need no one, for she would be complete.

Eileen had been with a boy once – her cousin – when she was fourteen, and almost got there. Down the fields, it was. He'd touched her with it, she said, down there, but they hadn't gone all the way. She'd have felt too guilty. And then, somehow, she'd let slip to her Ma about it, and her Ma was disgusted with her. One of her own! She made Eileen go to confession, and promise never to do such a dirty thing again. Eileen had said then that she would wait for marriage; it would be worth it, she thought, to be respectable; she'd only regret it later if she gave in now.

But Noreen no longer cared about that. What would it be like? She had wondered many times. Would it hurt, be ecstatic? Would she bleed? Blood had coloured her dreams sometimes, and she would wake, sobbing, in the strange night.

She felt as if she were about to undergo an operation, rather than be initiated into the joys of sex. How different this from Eileen's dreams of sweet, untouched virgin brides and strong, experienced men, united in respectable marriage.

He couldn't get her pants down, and she had to wriggle to get them off. They were her old navy school pants (she'd no idea why she'd those on), and she was glad it was dark. Kenny lay on top of her and said she must spread her legs, which she did, obediently, and then he was fumbling and groping, pushing at her.

Oh, she could weep. How dare they do that to her! PJ, or the red van, or Kenny – they filled her with disgust and shame (just like her mother had told her), and the knowledge that there would be no wonderful revelation. There could not be, and she should have known it. Surely there could not be for him, either (unless men were really as different as they were made out to be – and she didn't want to believe that).

After a while of lying still in the darkness, her head crushed against the window and the smell of car seats, they scrambled up and pulled on discarded scraps of clothes again. They were both awkward in the cramped space. Kenny seemed embarrassed about the incident, and even apologized. Noreen was not sure what for, exactly. She didn't care. She was empty. She cried, when he was gone, but her tears were not even full; they were empty too.

6

She never went to the dances again. Of late the magic had gone, anyhow; the dance-halls seemed dead and coarse, the passion of 'The Sash' futile and vulgar. Kenny argued halfheartedly with her, threatened suicide, then left. She never saw him again, apart from once, two years later, just before she went away. He drove by in the red Toledo, the radio blaring through the open window, some girl with curly brown hair beside him.

It was a strange, rootless time for Noreen, after Kenny. She felt oddly disconnected at times, and it seemed as if she saw people in a different way; more compassionately perhaps. It was as if she stood more outside herself, like once before –

There had been a bomb on the main road. She remembered it – wee Arty was driving the school bus that day, the cap askew over his weather-burnt face, and he cursed as he jammed on the brakes. Some traffic jam, they thought. But then there was this policeman running up the road, waving his arms and yelling, 'Get the hell out, get the hell out!' Noreen saw the terror in the policeman's face, and she knew then that she, Noreen Logan, a wee girl with brown hair tied back in a pony tail and a gorse house down the fields – that she would die one day. People would hear it on the news as they munched their bacon and eggs for tea, and then they'd change the channel and watch the film instead.

They were up the road by the time the bomb went off, and Arty took them into school by the motorway. He wouldn't let Noreen stand up at the front beside him, like he usually did, and she sat quiet, looking out of the window at the bare mountain with the TV pole on, and feeling that something had changed in her.

Sometimes now it seemed as if she had a clock in her head, ticking slowly, so slowly, it was unbearable. So many seconds, minutes, hours, days, weeks, years to fill. A lifetime could be long. She felt as if the clock must explode, wanted to scream, but didn't, for fear of what Ma would say.

She threw herself into her work, even stayed late in school sometimes. There was vague talk about exams, university; even going away, something which she had never imagined. It didn't mean much, at the moment. But still, it gave her something to aim at, some goal, for otherwise there was nothing. Life had never seemed so pointless. It was only the depression after Kenny, she told herself, even though she hadn't loved him, even though she knew it was more. But she couldn't pin it down.

After school she mooched about the shops in Belfast. The birds flew about the top of the white city hall in the early dusk, filling her throat with tears as she walked along in the dark, rushing crowds, anonymous. She went slowly, looking in all the windows, passing the paper-boy on the corner, who yelled, *Telegraph!* The queues at the checkpoints, clattering over the boards with their bags open, and then the bus station, the clock above one of the arched stands, and the great buses roaring out into the streets. Cigarette smoke in your nostrils in the cold evening. It came to her then that she would leave – next year, the year after, whenever; she would leave.

The last bus went at 5.20 from stand eight.

'Noreen!'

She turned round, and it was Paul Megarry standing behind her, holding his guitar case. He wore a brown leather jacket and a yellow scarf muffled round his neck. She could see the tip of his nose red with the cold, his breath hanging in the air.

'On your way home?'

She nodded, stamped her feet. She was conscious all of a sudden of her school uniform. He was tall, and she had to look up at him to speak. 'You?'

He was going to his parents' house. 'I have to be out there at weekends, because of the meetings, you know.'

She changed the subject, embarrassed. 'You work in Belfast, then?'

He taught in the Protestant boys' grammar – English and RE. He led the Christian group in his lunch hour, and some weekends he organized trips into the Mournes, where the boys stayed in crude huts and walked and climbed and sang. During the week he lived in a flat in Rugby Terrace, a few avenues along from Noreen's school. 'That's near you isn't it?'

She nodded, glancing up at him in the half-light of the station. She was aware of his closeness – the dark, almost Jewish face, the long nose, the blue eyes that startled you with their intensity.

'Exams this year?' he asked her.

'Well – next. The important ones, anyway.'

'So. What about after? After school. What then?'

She told him about university – maybe. A dream she had to travel. She didn't know why she told him. But he nodded, seemed to understand what she explained with difficulty – how she ached to learn, to live in far-away places, engulfed by strange languages; how she ached – to know . . . Things which she hadn't shared with anyone before, apart from in idle passing with Eileen, who always seemed to understand her half-yearnings and longings.

Then the bus roared into the stand, the brakes farted, and the doors flew open.

'I have to go now.'

He stood there still, looking at her. 'If you ever wanted to pop round,' he was saying, 'for some coffee, or to study, if you wanted . . . It's very quiet in the flat . . .' He cleared his throat. It was strange to see him embarrassed. She felt as if here might be the beginning of something – no. She shied away from it. He was so old, anyway.

'Here – I have to go.'

He stood at the bottom of the steps. 'How about Saturday night, Noreen? You're missed, you know.'

She hesitated. 'Well, maybe. I'll have to see how my work is.'

'It'll be in the green hall,' he shouted to her. 'We're having a speaker. Eight o'clock.'

He waved as the bus jerked out on to the road. She leaned her head back against the seat, thankfully – she didn't want to be involved – gazing out on to the darkening streets that were filled with people hurrying home from work, on foot, in cars, in buses. Her reflection gazed back at her from amongst the flickering lights of the bus, mirror of a future where she would sit in foreign, dimly lit places.

Getting off the bus in the cold dark and tramping down home between the hedges, all that passed from her. The city filled her with a sadness, a restlessness, almost a nostalgia, but for something which she had not yet experienced. Home was so familiar – too familiar. Ma was getting the bacon and eggs, her face a bit pinched looking. Tired. Her hair was newly permed, too tight, making her unusually severe. Her eyes flickered at Noreen as she came in the door, with a sort of nervousness, an uncertainty. It seemed as though Noreen, with her certainty (and yet it wasn't really certainty; she just made it seem like that) obliterated them. Da, with his comfortable belly, frowning at the paper through gilt-framed glasses. He smiled up at her, anxious to please.

'Good day?' She shrugged, inexplicably irritated as she closed the door on him.

The maddening thing was that she couldn't stop thinking about it – the meeting – even though she was sure she despised all that: repenting and crucifixion, salvation and living for ever. Yet she had realized with great clarity that time of the bomb scare that she would die one day. And then? Well, of course she couldn't believe all that stuff about eternal light and angels and harps. She didn't know what then.

She dreamt one night that she died. She didn't know how, in the dream; that wasn't really important. But she died, and had the sensation of her soul, or her spirit, whatever it was – anyway, her, the real her – moving out. She passed through this long, dark tunnel, which was her body, and then floated free. It was a weird feeling. She woke up afterwards and lay there in the dark, peaceful. It had been a pleasant experience, not like some of her other dreams, which made her wake yelling and frantic for the light.

Oh, she knew that she had sinned, been wicked; that hers was the path to Hell. It had never bothered her before, but all of a sudden it did. That one thing, especially, which she would rather not remember: the thing which happened in the dark of the house, with Eileen.

It had happened the summer when they were ten and had just left primary school. Everything had seemed different then. Ma had been unlike herself, after Granny dying, and, to help lift the depression, she took back her old job at the barracks in town. She worked in the offices, doing something with bills for soldiers who had to have repairs done on their houses. Each morning she went away with Da in the car, all smart in her stockings and high heels, and smelling of unaccustomed perfume, rushing about getting the breakfast and the packed lunches and putting the cats out. Noreen was old enough to look after herself now, they considered. Oh, she was eager to.

Ma didn't get in till late, and Noreen had to have the potatoes done and the place tidied round a bit. In winter she set the fire, though they wouldn't let her light it. She liked to be in the house on her own, though she did get a bit lonely before they came in, sometimes; but most days Eileen came back with her, and they never let on to anyone. At least they weren't running off down the fields, anyway – not much of the time.

The holidays drew near, and there was a sort of carefree feeling in the air. Nothing seemed to matter much, not even in school. They all felt happy, crazily happy, for there was nothing to dread, only the summer stretching before them, on and on until September.

There was a school outing to the coast on the last day before the end of term. They swam in the sea and went on the amusements, especially the big dipper, until all their money was gone. They went there on the train, and they could peer into people's back gardens, where the washing hung and only corrugated iron or wire fences separated them from the railway line. They could see kids playing around rusty old cars and women gossiping over back fences. In one place there was a great cemetery with thousands of graves in it, all with white headstones. Noreen had never dreamt before that there could be so many dead people. And then there was the sea, blue and glinting and glittering, and sunshine and straw hats and ice-cream and Barney's Amusements. There were hamburgers and fizzy drinks, the dodgems banging and sand between their toes when they got back on the train.

Then it was the end of term, and Eileen went away on holiday down South, like she did every year. There was a strange feeling of waiting. Noreen sat in the empty house, listening to silent breathing and heartbeat, until Ma came in from work and made the place chatter again. Or she sat outside in the garden beneath the apple tree from which the sun dripped like warm dew. Bees swarmed around a hive near the roof of the cottage, and their steady droning made her feel drifting and drowsy. You could see the heat shimmering, actually trembling in a sky of burning blue; Noreen floated in it, humming with the bees. She would awake to find shadows, and her legs red below her shorts. She got up, feeling herself sear with the late, lazy afternoon, lifting her bare feet quickly from the heat and dying bees. Then the house enfolded her in its dark, still insides, and she waited again within its cool stone and emptiness.

After two weeks Eileen returned from her holidays in the South, and they began a waiting game of another sort. It was appropriate, somehow, to that summer of curious suspension, of sharp bright and dark.

Eileen came to Noreen's house every day, and together they cut up pieces of card into squares, marking the letters of the alphabet on them with black ink. Then two more, one marked YES and the other marked NO. They got the wee round table from the good room, where the settee was immaculate and ornamental plates regimented the walls. Ma had recently had some travelling man polish and treat the table, so that its smooth mahogany glinted darkly (she still complained about the price, though). They placed the squares of alphabet round this with YES and NO opposite each other. Finally, they took a sherry glass from the cupboard in the kitchen, rubbed it with a cloth until it shone, then set it upside down in the middle of the table. Noreen had wanted to use something else, for her Ma would have killed her if she'd known they were using the best glasses, but Eileen insisted that only the best would do.

They sat down opposite each other, both touching the

glass lightly with one finger. Noreen all at once felt an irresistible urge to giggle, but Eileen sat solemn as one of those priests who hear your confession, and she suppressed it. The room breathed so quietly that they could hear the carriage clock ticking next door. It seemed that the silence itself ticked.

'Spooky, Spooky, is anyone there?' Eileen inquired, her voice rising on the last word. Noreen wanted to giggle again.

'Spirit of the Glass, are you there?' This time it was a low wail, which discomfited Noreen.

The glass brooded silently, as if intuiting Noreen's lack of faith. But Eileen stared grimly at it, finger never moving, until at last it ventured across the table, agonizingly slowly, but moving. That was the end of Noreen's disbelief.

'What is your name?' asked Eileen clearly, as if talking to a deaf person.

The glass was still.

'Your name?'

Noreen's finger trembled slightly on the glass.

Then she felt it move beneath her finger. Slowly at first, then quicker, as if becoming more sure of itself.

R – O – B – A – R – T

'Robert!' said Eileen triumphantly.

'It can't spell properly,' said Noreen.

'Shh!' said Eileen. 'You'll offend it.'

She concentrated on the glass again. 'What's your second name?'

W – I – L – L – There it stopped.

'Must be William,' said Eileen. 'Wouldn't you think? Here – you ask it something, Noreen.'

106

'Oh, no. I'd rather not.'

'Ach, go on! Ask it if it knows your Granny.'

'No, I will not!' That would have been going too far, somehow; the last step before something awful which she could not name.

'Ask it something, well!'

'All right!'

Noreen hesitated. Cleared her throat. Then, 'Spirit of the Glass, where are you?'

She heard Eileen suck in her breath.

The glass was silent for perhaps a whole minute.

'It's not going to answer,' said Eileen with relief.

'That was a stupid thing to ask it, Noreen!'

But then the glass began to move, swiftly and purposefully. She had known inside herself what the answer would be, but to have it spelt out . . . No mistakes this time.

H – E – L – L

The forbidden word pierced with a cold exhilaration.

'It can't mean it, though,' said Eileen, and she was pale. 'I'll ask it again. Hmm. Are you in a nice place?'

Whoosh. NO.

Their hearts ticked with the carriage clock, and their hands were clammy.

Other children played in the sun.

Then the spirit became agitated. The glass slid about the table at an alarming rate, spluttering nonsense, until Noreen feared that it would fall on the floor and shatter, and their world with it. For such an occurrence must surely have a terrible significance; and there was the scolding of her Ma to reckon with too. They lifted it from the smooth surface and put it away for that day.

But the thing worked. There was no doubt about that. Eileen's Ma read the tea leaves, after all, and they had both promised faithfully that neither of them would ever move the glass purposely; it spoke only of its own accord.

They were both afraid, though, even Eileen. She dreaded not least what her Ma would say if she found out, and wondered if she couldn't tell by looking in the teacups after dinner. One day something awful must happen; surely God would eventually strike them down with a pious thunderbolt, and righteousness would be restored. There must be some consequence – Noreen almost hoped that there would be, for otherwise the Devil prevailed.

Yet the game drew them, and there was no God or guilt when the glass moved. On other days they rarely had to wait. The glass would glide across the table, swiftly and purposefully, on the first invocation. They conversed at various times with Robert, a William (the same one?) and some colonel whose name they couldn't make out from the jumble of letters. Odd that they were all men. Noreen wondered if the Colonel was something to do with Ma working in the barracks. It must all have a meaning.

The glass, they were convinced, must know all secrets: of past, present, future. Oh, how they longed to know the future! Their future. They were greedy for knowledge.

'Will I be married?'

'Will we get our exams?'

'Go to grammar school?'

'Who will I marry?'

108

'When?'

'Will we still be friends?'

The glass, made slow by splinters of wills and shalls and Is, seemed reluctant – or could it possibly be unable? – to give concrete answers. It must know, though; it knew everything. Noreen and Eileen were sure of it. But the glass merely whirled nonsense, playing a game of its own, of which neither Noreen nor Eileen knew the rules. Or perhaps there were none. They feared that: this unknown.

'We should let it talk about itself more,' Noreen suggested once. 'About its life . . .'

They had tried that once before, near the beginning, but the glass had become agitated, too near the edge, and they had stopped. Now Eileen shook her head dangerously, and Noreen was glad. For they could only get in deeper and deeper, become drawn down into the eternal nothingness of that 'not nice' place. Anything could happen, and they loved and feared this anything.

As the bright days, which glinted harshly through the inner darkness, drew on, the spirits wearied. Robert and William often claimed exhaustion, and the glass lay still. But the Colonel became vociferous, saying more than Eileen would have allowed, had she had the power.

On one particular, frenzied day, he spelt out obscenities – such suggestions, they recalled later, unwillingly (they'd never dreamt . . .) – until at last he blasted with deafening silence;

Y - O - U - G - O - T - O - H - E - L - L

They didn't know whether it was a curse or a prediction; it didn't matter – the words were equally dreadful. The glass fell to the floor, where it lay brooding, terrible, but it did not break. Noreen and Eileen fled the dark, hypnotic room and ran into the bright, safe day, where others chased, dared, boasted.

That was the last time they played.

The cottage was changed, after that, for Noreen. She could no longer enjoy its silence, nor inhabit its dark, secret womb as she used to. Now the darkness held terror for her; she was always afraid of some other being which loured in that stillness. The smooth, round table accused her from the sombre good room, and the glass in the cupboard shivered her. The silent rooms pounded in her head, until she had to escape outside.

One day she burnt the alphabetic, prophetic cards on the fire in a sort of mystic, hopefully exorcizing ritual. But her stomach still chilled in the house, like frozen giblets caged in a supermarket cabinet. She could not bear to be alone in it.

Then it happened that Da went away over the water on business for a few days, and Ma had a card evening arranged with Big Iris and the other girls from her office. There were four of them who worked together: Big Iris and Ma, Ella and Minnie Stewart. They took their packed lunches together and went out for a treat to McCauley's whenever it was someone's birthday. They took it in turns to have the card evenings in each other's houses, about once every three weeks or so. Sometimes, like around Christmas time, the men came too, and they partnered each other for whist, but most often it was just the women who played. They played knockout whist then, and Twenty-ones, throwing their coppers in to the middle of the table. There would be a big supper laid on: sandwiches and éclairs and pavlova, when it was in the

Logans' house. Noreen got to finish up the bits after-wards, or at the very least to lick the bowls when Ma was doing the baking. Sometimes there would even be a chicken casserole with rice, and pineapple delight to follow. Big Iris would be all dressed up in one of her large flowered dresses, which she belted at the middle, beneath her immense bust. Her teeth stuck out, and sometimes the bright red lipstick smudged down on to them, especially when she bit into one of Ma's cream-filled éclairs, and the sweet stuff splurged out both sides of her mouth. Big Iris loved to talk, to know everything about everyone and to tell it too. She had a great laugh, and her whole body used to shake as she rocked about on her chair.

Then there was Ella, but there was nothing much to say about Ella; she was a pleasant woman who dressed neatly and had a patent-leather handbag. Minnie was small and gave you the impression of being dried up somehow; as if Iris, with her flowing, luxurious figure, had used up all the good things and there were none left for Minnie. Minnie had a wart on her cheek, and she had lost two babies. Her eyes stared through thick glasses, as if she just couldn't fathom the world. She went on about her illnesses – Ma said she was a hypochondriac – and the other three exchanged conspiratorial glances behind her back. She complained about the food when-ever they went out to McCauley's, and she couldn't take Ma's chicken casserole because it was sweet and sour, and she said it repeated on her. Still, they always asked her along, and they must have been quite fond of her really.

The women chattered and laughed on those evenings –

oh, until way into the night. You could tell they were glad because the men weren't there. They were different somehow, without the men: as if they didn't have to be on their best behaviour any more. They were sort of closer and freer, stronger together. It was like the feeling of truancy which Noreen used to have with Ma when they ate blackberries on their way home from church in the autumn: snatched moments of forbidden intimacy which made Noreen excited and curious as she lay in bed on those nights.

She couldn't stop Ma from going now. They were to play cards at Big Iris's.

'I'd stay home, if you'd rather,' said Ma. Noreen could tell she was unwilling.

'Oh no,' Noreen replied automatically. 'Sure Eileen could come,' she added, half hoping Ma would say no.

'Oh aye.' Ma was relieved. 'Ask Eileen. Don't mention it to your Da, though,' she said, as an afterthought.

So Eileen came, reluctantly, to keep Noreen company. Ma stood by the door, saying things like, don't forget to lock the door after me, don't stay up too late! She had on her make-up and her best paisley dress beneath her cream coat. She smelt of perfume. She kissed Noreen before she went out the door, and Noreen almost pleaded, 'Don't go!' as if she were a wee girl again. But Ma waved through the window, and then she was gone.

At least it didn't get dark too early these late-summer days. It wasn't so bad while the light was there. But it seeped away, slowly, insidiously, until it was quite gone. They watched the television until the programmes were finished for the evening, then they made a huge supper of weak tea and toasted Veda bread, dripping with butter. They tried the radio, but it would only crackle, and they switched it off again. The house lay quiet with that quietness which houses have at night: doors shuddering, ceilings cracking, windows tapping. It was alive, the house.

And the table was just in the next room, the glass in the cupboard. Mustn't think of that. They considered more food, but neither of them had any appetite. Besides, they were scared to go out into the kitchen, where the windows were bare and dark, and the night could see in.

The fire had died down to a few dully glowing embers, which sighed away into dust in the grate. Noreen and Eileen sat in silence, secretly anxious as the wind scratched at the door, or the dog whined for no apparent reason. If they didn't think about it, then it wouldn't happen; but what else was there to think about?

They waited in silence. If only Ma would come home, then everything would be all right; normality would be restored. They sat, willing it, but only the ashes blew, and the dog moaned with the wind.

And then they heard it. The sharp, unmistakable click of the front door opening and closing. They gazed at the fear in each other's faces and could not move. They remained sitting, powerless, riveted to each other's eyes by terror.

Then at last there was Noreen's Ma and everything suddenly familiar again. Scoldings for staying up late – sure they were white with exhaustion! They had to go to bed and listen to the house again. They lay rigid, listening, dozing off every now and then, only to wake with a start in the darkness.

Eileen left, thankfully, before breakfast, saying she'd some messages to do for her Ma first thing.

They never mentioned that night when they saw each other again. Nor the spirit of the glass. They would rather pretend it had never happened.

Eileen attended chapel regularly for a while, beneath her Ma's suspicious eye, and eased her conscience with Hail Marys. But there was no such consolation to be found in Noreen's Church – only the assurance that the wicked would burn in the fires of Hell.

7

That Saturday Da drove her through the mist to the wee Evangelical Mission Hall over the hill. It was just as she remembered it: the green corrugated iron of it standing like a cowshed in the middle of the fields, filling you with a sort of a pity for humanity, its puny strivings and consolations.

'God bless you, love,' said Da, before he drove off.

Noreen frowned. She did not like to be blessed.

Inside it was more bare than she remembered: the floorboards, the primitive benches, the boards on the walls. But the windows were flimsily curtained now, and there were some posters on the walls. She looked at those while she was waiting for everything to begin. She felt conspicuous sitting there, not knowing anyone, apart from the girl with brown hair, Rosalind, who smiled at her. She wished for a cigarette or a drink.

One poster was of a large, bright candle, beneath which was written, 'Behold, I am the light of the world!'

She looked at that for a long time. 'I' presumably meant Jesus. But which world was He the light of? Surely not of this one, not of Noreen's world, where people fought and killed and hated. There was no Jesus here.

Grandma was the only dead person Noreen knew. She had always seemed old, Granny McCready, ever since Noreen could remember, with her white hair in a bun and the pains in her face. Once she lived up a bumpy old lane in the Dromara hills, with cats on the chairs and scones warm from the oven, but then she went to live with other old people in the town; they wouldn't let her stay alone any more.

Noreen remembered going to visit her at the top of a dirty-red brick house with long windows like watching faces. They climbed stairs which were dark with shadows, and they heard birds cackling behind doors (old people had to have something, Ma said). Caged birds and age – the place gave you the creeps. And at the top was Grandma, whose flat smelt funny and who called Noreen 'Nonie'. There was a golliwog thing holding a tray in a corner, and it looked at Noreen with a grin on its face. There was something sinister about it, and Noreen asked to go to the bathroom, but that was worse, with a huge claw-footed bath and a mangle and a cupboard which had doors reaching all the way up to the ceiling. The loo had a long chain instead of a handle, and Noreen ran out quick when she'd flushed it because of the noise and the dark in there and what might be in the cupboard. After that she kept close to Ma on the couch, which miraculously folded down into a bed for them to sleep on that night.

Granny McCready was soft and large compared to Granny Logan, with her wiry permed hair and good dresses. Noreen saw Granny McCready with her poor white hair let down when she was ready for bed in a nightdress which had ties under the chin, and she had no teeth, so that it was hard to make out what she said. She held a soft towel up to her face as if it would comfort her, but it didn't, for she still closed her shrivelled eyelids from time to time and then had to go to bed, for she was so tired.

There was a green budgie in a cage which showed off and swung about on one foot and said 'Pretty Joey' in a cackly voice. Noreen stood talking to it while Ma cleared up the lunch things (ham and salad – she hated it), then it pecked her finger and she yelled. Ma asked her crossly what was she doing, and Grandma summoned her over to her great soft chair and gave her a banana, which seemed right somehow.

One of the nicest things about the visit was that it was Sunday, and Noreen missed going to Sunday school. There was even a wee shop on the corner of the street that was open and selling papers and sweets, and Noreen was allowed to go and get some sweets, so long as she didn't tell her Da. When she came back, Ma and Grandma were having an argument, but they stopped when Noreen came in. She just heard the tail-end of it – Grandma saying that she wouldn't be a burden on anyone, and she was too old for change anyhow. Ma and Noreen went soon after that, and the golliwog's leer pricked Noreen in the back. She felt sorry for Grandma, all alone with it.

She asked Ma if she could stop going to Sunday school altogether, and what the golliwog thing was. Ma said that she could do whatever she wanted (but she didn't mean it really). Her voice sounded all funny. Then she wiped her eyes and said that the golliwog thing was called a dumbwaiter, which seemed appropriate, for it did look dumb – but sinister. Grandma had looked out at them from the tall window of the tall house, and the next thing she was dead.

Noreen tried to imagine her, soft and white and tooth-less and holding the pains in her face, up in Heaven with God, living eternally in warm, loving light, but she couldn't. No, Heaven, if it existed, was surely not for people like that; not for ordinary people who lived in the world.

Where, then, was it – this light, which Jesus was sup-posed to be? Perhaps poor Malcolm had a bit of it, run-ning through the fields like a tree-child. It said somewhere in the Bible that Christians must be as little children. But Noreen felt that what was in Malcolm was more of a darkness, such as was in the land; you could feel it sometimes, in the loughs and bogs and hills.

Then of course there was Da, and Granny Logan. But Granny Logan fussed and complained, like any other elderly woman. Surely there was no radiance in her. Da read the Bible and tried to live in the way which he thought right; but he was just Da, after all. They lived too closely: their encounters were everyday.

Paul arrived and smiled at her across the room, as he took his guitar out of its case, and the meeting began. He introduced the speakers, an American missionary and his wife, who had long, long hair and a calm, lovely face. They spoke of Jesus in a way which Noreen had never heard before: they spoke not about right and wrong, but about love, what you spent your whole life searching for, in some form or other. Marriage and chil-dren and friends, houses and gardens – it was all a search for love, fulfilment, meaning.

And now here was Jesus, the answer to all that – the answer to your hopelessness, your lostness. Noreen was lost, at the moment, without Kenny, whom she did not love, but she ached anyway; without Eileen; without Ma and Da, who were strangers to her. Not just those tangible things, though, oh, there was more, she ached and was lost but could not express it – so many intangible things, which she half glimpsed and wept over but could not quite catch.

Jesus, they said, will give your life meaning, if you let Him. He will warm your aching, fill you up with love, which is what you yearn for, secretly, what we all yearn for.

Don't reject His love, as you did before, as we all did! We all rejected it; crucified Jesus. But his love is so vast, so vast, that He is giving us another chance.

It was almost as if He spoke to her Himself. I suffered this agonizing death for you, Noreen. You rejected me and crucified me – you, whom I had come to save, to love. You spat on me and drove nails through my hands and feet, letting me die slowly, so slowly. You killed me, all because you wouldn't listen . . .

He just wouldn't stop talking to her. And His voice was so gentle (like Paul's). She thought she could see His eyes, full of compassion and suffering. Oh, she'd crucified Jesus a thousand times already in the course of her short life; she did see that. Not so much because of what she'd done – stolen and lied, drunk and danced, been easy with men, connived with the Devil (oh, the very worst!) – but because of what she hadn't done. It was plain to her now: she hadn't loved. It came upon her all of a sudden, left her devastated. It wasn't the sinning that was important; no, no. Oh, God. It was the love.

Noreen looked around at the Jesus-people, and they

gleamed and shone. Jesus loved them, they loved Him, and they would live and love eternally. For them, there was no uncertainty. They were the Blessed of the world!

She wanted this love. Oh, she did.

The choice is yours, said Jesus. You can believe, and be saved; or doubt, and be damned. God is an infinitely fair God, who will never force anyone. The choice is yours. You can have freedom of thought, but you'll have to pay for it.

All she wanted was love, though. No Heaven or Hell, just love. And, strangely, beauty.

Jesus is love, they said.

Surely she had always seen this moment. For hadn't God always been there – in the hills, in Sunday school, even in Eileen's chapel, which she had attended once. It seemed to her now that she had always known, secretly, that one day she would have to pay attention to those challenges, to the writing nailed to trees and old men's backs; that one day there must be a reckoning, a sacrifice, a commitment. Just the time had never been right.

Oh, how grand, how deep, how meaningful, to suffer for a cause! To be tried, tested, burnished – to have meaning. To dart through life like a burning arrow. It seemed that everything – but everything – in life had prepared her for this moment; always, only this moment. Until, brought to sacrificial maturity, she was ripe to be popped into the mouth of God.

Noreen returned home from the green hall a new woman. Luckily her Ma and Da were in bed, so she didn't have to confess to anyone. She slept soundly, and awoke the next morning feeling remarkably the same.

She stared at herself in the mirror when she got up, expecting to see the new person who had been 'born-again'. But the outside looked just the same, and she feared that there was just her inside too. Just her.

She wasn't quite sure what she had expected, anyway, only that there ought to be some sort of immediate and drastic change, after Paul had said the short, earnest prayer with her beneath the stars outside the green hall in the fields. Something must happen.

He gave her a lift home on the back of his motorbike, and they flew through the universe along dark, country roads. He warned her, in that so gentle voice which he used to speak to his Lord, not to expect an overnight miracle, that these things took time; but still, Noreen was disappointed that there had been none.

How else, after all, could Jesus come into her heart? How else could she be born again? Surely lightning must flash, thunder rumble. Something . . .

She asked Jimmy McCormack on the way home from the bus stop: where was He, then – Jesus? They'd all sung, 'He's alive! Jesus is alive today!' But no one ever said where.

Jimmy said, in our hearts; everywhere! But some people can't see Him: non-Christians, that is. Anyway, she must ask Paul about it. He was good at explaining these things.

Paul smiled sympathetically at Noreen – his sister in the Lord, he called her – and told her that she mustn't play into the hands of the Devil (for a wild moment she wondered if he could possibly know about the spirit-raising sessions with Eileen). She mustn't fall into the trap of thinking too much.

'The Devil twists our thoughts and uses them to confuse us,' he explained gently. 'Undermining our faith in God. That's why the Lord prefers us simple, like children. We must just have faith. You know, Noreen, the wisdom of men is but foolishness in the eyes of God.'

Everything seemed so clear, so simple, when Paul explained it.

'Trust and believe,' his voice finished calmly, like a hymn, 'and He will do great things.'

Oh, she would try, she would try. There was nothing she wanted more than for God to do great things, through her, His new child, Noreen. She immersed herself in God's Word: every morning when she got up, every evening before she went to bed. How she loved the Bible, with its wealth of meaning; every sentence, every word was symbolic (why had she not seen it before?). All people must find themselves there.

She loved the analogies, the similes, the symbols of the Biblical language; the aptness of the 'born-again' analogy delighted her particularly: the fathering by the Holy Spirit, then the long pregnancy, during which growth and maturing took place, and finally the bursting out of the new person, which was you. There was a miracle after all: the miracle of birth.

She found such things again and again, little phrases that fitted her inner landscape exactly. She had no doubts that God knew her perfectly. And it was easy, then, to trust, to believe. She wanted so much to find 'true life'. Oh, give me meaning, purpose, and I will die for it! It was not the stark contrast of right and wrong, of sin and repentance, that moved her; rather the lascivious promise of joy, love, fruitfulness; the overwhelming desire to be engulfed, to bathe in God, who was Life.

She took up Paul's offer and visited his flat in Belfast after school one day. The other fellows smiled at her over their mugs of coffee, and Paul whisked her off quickly into his room, blushing. Such a talk they had: of the Christian life, of spiritual warfare with the Devil, of the need for fellowship – oh, so much. They even prayed together, on Paul's suggestion, and she did not find it too painful; she was not embarrassed with him. Afterwards, Noreen walked down the avenue beside the school, where the chestnut trees dropped dry leaves which cracked beneath her feet. The sky was a cold, fragile blue, and she could see her breath. She felt happy; so happy.

It seemed that life all of a sudden was ripe with blessings. God had given so much. The believers, said the Bible, will drain the cup of beauty and mystery, which will yet continue to flow in never-ending abundance. They will live always in the land that abounds with milk and honey. They are like trees planted by rich streams, and out of their hearts shall flow rivers of living water.

But this new life was not all honey and living water. It demanded also sacrifice, discipline, rigour. The Lord who promised fruitfulness, bounty, everlasting life, also demanded that she deny not only her own self, but mother, father, sister, brother, friends, for His sake. She was not quite sure of the implications of it all yet. She only knew that she must take up her cross; she must sacrifice her life in order to find it.

She learned that only the weak and meek were fit for the Kingdom of Heaven, for only in such could God display His power. Those who were strong in their own right counted for nothing in God's world, for there was no room in such people for Himself. Their very strength condemned them. This was a hard lesson to learn.

By myself I am nothing, nothing.

Noreen repeated this constantly. I am nothing. Pride must be rooted out, along with other defective feelings. She had no worth, save that which being Christian gave her; she must have no confidence in herself, but rely totally on God. Her weakness would be her strength. Negative would be made positive. It was so paradoxical – and so lovely.

Only such self-denial made possible envelopment by the beloved, which was the prime aim. 'I' ceased to be; God, Jesus, Spirit, became all. Self disappeared; instead there was fusion with Christ – the symbolic sharing in His crucifixion and ascension. You were a part of Him. He was your life. Noreen believed that she loved Him.

She took on the burden of praying for souls to be saved; all, all must find the right way – the way of the born-again. She prayed for the girls in school, who pointed the finger and laughed behind her back ('Noreen's changed, you know!'), and for her former best friend, Eileen. She prayed for her mother, who spoke of the dangers of her 'sudden religious fervour' and worried about fanaticism. Ma had no understanding.

'Why must you be so extreme?' she complained, as Noreen set off for the meeting one night, Bible under arm. (Paul had given it to her; it was made of black leather, with fine crinkly pages, and inside was written, 'God bless you, Noreen. All my love in our Lord, Paul'.

'It's not natural,' said Ma, 'for a young girl like you – always going to meetings and praying. All things in moderation!'

Noreen explained patiently that religion wasn't something you did on just one day of the week; it was a way of life – what you lived for, indeed.

Ma shook her head grimly and set about the washing-up, crashing the dishes. She wished Noreen would go to the dances again – those were certainly the lesser of the two evils. At least there she might meet some nice fellow . . .

Even her Da – even he spoke of opinions; of tolerance, freedom of thought. There were many great religions in the world, and, even if he didn't agree with them, he respected them. 'God means many different things to many different people,' he said quietly, 'and that is the only reason He can exist at all.'

Da's religion was essentially private, just between himself and God. It was extended, at most, to his family, by way of his prayers. He failed to see the greater purpose in evangelizing the world. Noreen was disappointed by what she saw as his lack of strength, his lack of vision. For she had a belief that burned. There could only be one way, one belief, one God. To compromise, to admit other views, was to betray the cause. Did not God spew out the lukewarm? What excruciating ecstasy to have to recognize the Devil in one's own parents.

She prayed for them.

Noreen worshipped the Lord in the tiny green mission hall in the fields, in church, and in other people's houses. Rosalind, with her lovely brown eyes, became a special friend; they sat together in the meeting, shared their problems, prayed for each other. They even wrote each other little letters of encouragement during the week which they spent apart – verses which the Lord had laid upon their hearts.

> I will lift up mine eyes to the hills,
> From whence doth my help come?
> My help comes from the Lord
> Who made heaven and earth.

And then there was Paul, of course. It was with Paul that she first went to the great hall in Belfast, and it was there that she touched depths which she had never imagined existed – the baptism in the Spirit.

Those who were already baptized had eyes which shone, and they hugged each other without awkwardness. They lifted their hands when they worshipped God, and the rest of the fellowship frowned upon them. It was an exciting time for the dissidents, and Paul, the leader, was in the forefront of it all. He did not want to influence Noreen, he told her, worried; her actions must come from the Lord. She must search her heart about baptism. Oh, but she had no doubts; she would take all, all that God had to offer.

A man with bald head, and eyes that shone too, stood up at the front of the packed hall and read from the Bible. On the day of Pentecost, so it went, a mighty rushing, like wind, filled the house where the Apostles sat, and tongues of flame rested on their heads. This was the coming of the Spirit, which God had promised after Jesus' ascension into Heaven. It meant that the power of God had really come upon His people, and this power was to be manifested by the gifts of the Spirit: prophecy, speaking in tongues, healing the sick and other miracles.

There was talk of being drunk with the Spirit, and dancing before the Lord. And Noreen saw it: the people dancing in the aisles to guitars and cymbals, abandoning themselves to adoration of God. It was something of which she had never dreamt, and she was sure that this was her destiny. For this she had been waiting all her life: for possession by God, for the deepest experience. How she longed for abandonment, immersion, drowning in the ocean of God.

The bald man laid hands on her head and spoke in strange tongues. As he did so, Noreen felt a peace come into her. Spirit, love, joy – these things possessed her mind. She whispered, moaned with the others, 'You're beautiful, Jesus!' Everyone felt it. You belonged, for everyone believed and felt as one. You were carried away on a wave of Jesus. That was all there was.

Some stood, eyes raised, arms raised, to Jesus; others sat, eyes closed, lips blissful. They all thought the same thing. Noreen felt it, like a current buzzing, but silently, in the great hall. Never had she known such harmony. Time ceased. The Beloved, Jesus, is here; we see Him. We love you, Jesus, Rose of Sharon, Lily of the Valley. We adore you, worship you. You are everything to us.

She could have cried, because her love, their love, was so overwhelming. They were all united; strong, because together. They drowned in their belief. There were songs swelling dark and keen in a wild love-chant: esoteric, passionate. You were swept away. Guitars wept, sensuous, then there were tambourines and hand-clapping, urgent. The dancing in the aisles was rapturous, signalling the imminent climax of intoxication. And finally, finally, came the state of transport, ecstatic union of the soul with God.

The Jesus-people and Noreen now enjoyed perfect, unimpeded communication with Jesus. They were in Him, He in them. It was so perfect, so whole.

The worshippers, who were now God, spoke in dark languages. God's people will live for ever, they prophesied. I will pour out My Spirit on all My people, they said. They cried the signs of the Second Coming: wars, fire, smoke, the sun turned to darkness, the moon to blood.

Only Noreen, who longed to so much, did not feel moved to speak in tongues. But her time would come; she believed that. For surely, surely this had been her destiny, even before she was squeezed from her mother's womb. God had known her then, even then. He knew the secrets of birth, of life, of death. He was meaning, wisdom, love: everything.

She was united with God's people, and they were right, she knew; God's people were right. And it was their duty to try and make other people see . . .

That year there was to be a summer mission against Catholicism down in the South of Ireland. Noreen was invited to join the group who were to go from the fellowship; even though so young in the Lord, she was considered to be strong already. It was what she had been waiting for: at last, the chance to fight for God, in a tangible way; to be properly fighting.

They had special meetings of preparation for it every Wednesday evening in the green hall. Paul came up specially from Belfast. Even though he was very tired by the end of the week, he did not complain; it was all work for the Lord.

Paul called Catholicism 'the dark enemy of our faith'. He went on about the mass, and the statues, and the candles which they lit for the dead. Noreen felt uneasy. The Catholics worshipped idols, Paul said, and had no assurance that they would go to Heaven. They relied mistakenly upon their own good works, rather than on the grace of God. And then the priests . . . Why did Jesus come to earth, if not to make direct intercession possible? And the Pope, clearly marked out by the Bible as the anti-Christ . . . All blasphemies, said Paul.

Noreen comforted herself with the thought that she had only been once to the mass. Only once, when she was wee. Perhaps it didn't matter too much . . . But she knew that it did. She shivered at her ignorance, at her sin. All blasphemies, Paul had said.

It was after Granny McCready had died. She had slept on a mattress on Eileen's floor that night, so that Eileen had to walk over the top of her, giggling, to get to the loo. You could hear voices from the next house – kids whingeing, and adults' voices raised, though you couldn't make out exactly what they said, and a bed creaking somewhere. It was all new and strange. Then gradually it all became quiet, apart from the occasional car roaring round the corner, doors slamming, voices and heels, then quiet again.

She remembered to mutter her Lord's Prayer, as Da liked her to. Eileen crossed her arms when she climbed into bed. She said that it was to gain indulgences.

'Oh.' Noreen wasn't any the wiser.

Then Eileen told about the Act of Contrition, and the prayer to stop you dying in your sleep.

'I don't believe all that stuff really, though,' she said.

Noreen was rather shocked. 'What d'you pray for, then?'

'Well, just in case . . .'

Eileen giggled. Then she started telling about her Granda, and how she'd seen him when he died. She told about the coffin with the ould man in it, and how she'd had to kiss him, and how a car had overtaken the funeral procession on its way to the church and that had a terrible, terrible meaning.

Noreen lay there in the dark, imagining what the terrible thing might be. She shivered. Eileen went on about how she'd dreamt that night that she was locked in the room with the dead man and couldn't get out. Noreen was glad she hadn't seen Grandma. She wished that it weren't so dark, and that Ma and Da were nearby. She felt uneasy in the strange house, with its unfamiliar noises and the disturbing holy pictures on the walls. She should have gone to Granny Logan's after all.

'We lit candles,' said Eileen into the dark. 'You pay to light candles for the dead, and it helps them get to Heaven.'

'Maybe,' Noreen ventured into the dark, 'maybe I could light one for Grandma.' She would so like to do something to help poor Granny McCready, with her soft white hair and the pains in her face. 'Have you got any?'

Eileen laughed. 'They're in chapel, stupid, with the priests. D'you want to confess as well?'

'Oh no,' said Noreen, 'I don't think I'd want to do

that.' She didn't like the idea of the priests, who listened and punished. She didn't want to tell them all the wrong things she'd done; it was better to keep all that to yourself, or else to tell it to God, who probably wasn't listening anyway.

The next day was Sunday, and she went to mass with Mrs McAllister and Eileen. It was great, because you didn't have to dress up, like for church. You could wear any old thing, and no one minded. The place was full of kids too.

Outside in the porch there was a font with holy water in it; you dabbed your fingers in and crossed yourself. Inside there were statues of tortured saints, all benign and bleeding beneath their robes, and people kneeling before them muttering, but you couldn't hear what they said. Noreen wondered if Granny McCready had prayed to the golliwog thing in her flat (she would have prayed to it; it was much more frightening than the Virgin Mary).

She glimpsed the cubicles with green curtains where people went to do their confessing. There was a window through which you whispered all your sins, and the priest sat listening on the other side. It was awful, Eileen said, because you were always afraid that the kids behind you in the queue would hear what you whispered. Then the priest gave you a penance, usually three Hail Marys, which didn't take very long to say, and you skipped out feeling wonderfully free and happy, until the sins started building up again.

Eileen curtsied to the front before she sat down, and Noreen copied her, though she couldn't see who she was curtsying to. Then the priest appeared from the vestry with the altar boys, all dressed in long robes that had white lacy stuff in. They all did their curtsy and proceeded up the aisle, carrying flickering candles and waving a thing that gleamed and gave out a lovely smell. Oh, it was a wonderful, exquisite experience! The scent and the robes and the flickering candles in dark corners; then the incantations, psalms and hymns, and you kneeled – there were wee red cushions to put your knees on.

The supreme moment was when the Host – she didn't know what it was exactly, only that it was very sacred and white – was revealed on the altar, and you didn't dare look. Eileen clasped her hands before her eyes. Mrs McAllister went up to the front with privileged others to partake of the white, fearful host, the body, which the priest put on your tongue. It was a ritual full of dark and mystery and a strange deep beauty which touched some hidden part deep inside of you.

Afterwards Noreen put her money into the box and lit a candle for Grandma. She watched it flicker, imagining the old lady herself flickering towards Heaven. She had a feeling somehow that her Da would have disapproved; but then he didn't need any help – he was saved already. She never told him about it, anyway.

Ma and Da were there waiting to take her home when she arrived back from the mass with Eileen and Mrs McAllister. It was only when she saw Da's face that she remembered she'd promised to go to the Methodist service with Granny Logan, who would meet her at the church and see her home again afterwards. Her sin – for surely it was sin – in attending the mass had caught up with her. She'd only wanted to light a candle for poor

Granny McCready, but she couldn't very well explain that to Da. Mrs McAllister fussed about and got them cups of tea. They looked very smart and well dressed amongst the kids in their old clothes, and Kathleen's new baby screaming. They sat on the sofa looking at the haloed Virgin Mary. You could hear Mr McAllister out the back somewhere, banging at some old bit of a car. Noreen suddenly felt ashamed that she was in her old comfortable clothes, and Grandma just dead.

She went up to Eileen's room to get her things, and they drove her away home in the car. Da drove without speaking. Noreen was afraid. She had never seen him like this before.

It was one of those days when it never got properly light all day; there was wind and driving rain, and then by half-past three or so night came down for good. There was a road block which Da didn't see in the strange dusk until they were almost on top of it. The soldiers loomed in at the window and swore at him and told him he almost got a bullet in his f—in' belly. Noreen crouched in the back. But the soldiers only looked in the boot and shone their torch at them through the rain, then waved them on. Da looked straight ahead and didn't speak, and you could almost see the anger sitting like a black cloud over his head, and him fighting it silently inside his head. Noreen knew that she had brought the whole thing upon them with her guilty sin, her mass, and she feared her father's anger and what she might have unwittingly done to Grandma by lighting the candle.

She was sent straight to bed when they got home. She could hear their voices from the sitting-room, Da's voice raised, and Ma's soft, tearful. She heard them mention 'the mass' and 'led astray'. The next morning Da said to her that she must never attend the mass again. He had nothing against the Catholics, but Noreen was a Methodist; the family were Methodist – that was their religion, their tradition. Ma looked pale, strained. Her eyes were red. Noreen knew that if it weren't for Ma, and Granny just having died, it would all have been much worse. She hadn't meant any harm, she told Da. They said no more about it. But Noreen lay there thinking for a long time that night – about the mass, and death. She still didn't understand the thing properly – what had happened to make Grandma dead. Life and death were a mystery to her, life a flame which flickered in the windy passages of your body like the candles in chapel. One day a breath would come along, just a bit stronger than the ones before, and snuff it out, into death, whatever that was. Blackness. It was a random process, and all you could do was go on lighting more candles.

Noreen determined then that she would take Ma away with her for ever, when she grew up. She would take her away and never let her die, like Grandma did.

8

The time for the mission had come. They drove down South in four cars, loaded up with tents and tins and Bibles. The small Christian army camped in a muddy field for two weeks and stewed up bacon and beans every night. Afterwards they sang and praised the Lord for His good works and got bitten by midges. They felt warm and good and blessed. And bitten – but that was all part of it; hardship enriched.

It would enrich others too; they were convinced of it. Every morning began with prayer for the souls who were on the brink of being saved, surely engaged at that very moment in a battle between good and evil.

There was wee Johnnie, for instance.

'Give him the courage, Lord, to suffer separation and hatred from family and friends, that he may live for ever as one of your children.'

So they prayed, fervently; they would have fought his battle for him, if they could, strong in their togetherness, in their righteousness. There was such agreement, such harmony, such collective feeling beneath the grimy canvas: how could they fail? How could they be wrong? They saw one thing only: God . . . their God.

Johnnie said a prayer and was born-again, much to the priest's disgust. The betrayed man came along to the camp, wild, white-haired, and the cross that hung round his neck trembled with passion. He was rather how Noreen imagined that God must have been in the Old Testament, when He was mighty with fire and appeared to people.

It would be poor Johnnie Reilly who would have to endure life here afterwards, said the godly man; he'd still be here, when his converters had gone back home. Did they not realize what they were doing?

The fellowship prayed for this wanderer too.

Johnnie was upset when they told him he'd have to stop praying to statues of saints and of the Holy Mary.

'But she's got such a lovely face,' he whimpered. 'And me sister's called Mary.'

'No, Johnnie,' said Paul firmly. 'It's blasphemy. Don't you know your commandments? Statues make God angry. D'you think He went to all the trouble of sending His beloved, His only Son to earth, to die in agony on the cross, just so you can pray to statues?'

Johnnie stared at the ground. 'Father McTaggart says . . .'

Paul shook his head quietly, smiling, but there was a hardness in his eyes which Noreen had not noticed before; something that would not give.

'Compromise,' he said, 'will be the ruin of any believer. Johnnie, it is the weapon of the Devil, can't you see that? There can be no middle way.'

Johnnie stood with bowed head.

'Pray to Jesus,' Paul said.

Noreen watched the child go, crying softly and clutching his rosary beads, with which he must also part.

It was quite an event, one way or another, when the mission arrived in the Southern village. The meetings were held in the market square, where farmers and sheep looked in, and housewives congregated for a daily yarn. And there were the holidaymakers too, fresh from the windy beaches. Most of all, though, it was the young ones, such as there were, who came in the evenings, for there was nothing else to do. Here was something, at least; people from another life. It gave them hope, of a sort. They heard the choruses and little plays with bewilderment, the talks by Paul with boredom, and the witnessing with the greatest glee.

This painful baring of souls was grand entertainment. An expectant hush, rippled with giggles, would fall, as the day's victims climbed the makeshift platform and recounted, blushing, how the Lord had saved them. They spoke of sin, repentance and new life; never before had this language felt so alien as it did now.

Noreen couldn't believe that her turn up there would ever come, the prospect appalled her so. She could hear Rosalind's quiet voice talking above her, and then the awful moment came when it stopped, and she was standing on the platform before the giggling faces; the thought that God could use her only when she was weak was of little comfort now. Her heart was rushing, and her voice sounded so strange. Surely it wasn't her voice.

'I used to drink and dance . . . I did awful things . . .' There was a titter in the audience. 'Until the Lord spoke to me. I tried not to listen but He went on speaking and He loved me so much . . . until I realized I was living in sin and He had come to save me, if only I would let Him and I gave my life to Him . . .'

Oh, how could she explain it? The love, the beauty. You got through these things somehow, even the worst things, like going to the dentist, or being caught stealing, or the hurt of other people, which you'd caused; they had to finish some time. She supposed that Hell must be when the things just went on and on and never finished.

'Thank you, Noreen.' Paul smiled at her, proud. He knew that it had been difficult for her; that she had won a battle. He had fought along with her, silently. She knew that. Of course, God had helped her through it. She thanked Him, and tried not to think about it any more. Of course He had been there. She climbed down from the platform gratefully, trying not to look at the faces which had witnessed her shame.

'Noreen!' It was a strangely familiar voice, which somehow should not have been there, not in that context.

She turned. It was Eileen McAllister standing there.

Eileen was eating an ice-cream – a Double 99, with the chocolate sucked away to two wee stumps.

'But what are you doing here?' They stood away from the crowd a bit.

'Oh, holidays,' Eileen replied vaguely. 'Sure we always come down South every year, for a couple of weeks. Don't you recall? My Ma has relatives in Drogheda . . . I'm down wi' Geraldine and Brendan.'

Eileen smiled slightly, in a puzzled sort of way. There were fresh freckles on her nose. She was wearing shorts and a t-shirt, which was flecked with sand, and Noreen felt frumpy in her decent summer dress.

'But tell me, Noreen,' she had another lick of the ice-cream, 'you haven't turned religious? Well, I suppose you must have.' She frowned. 'But then maybe you always were a bit like that, somehow . . . sort of quiet, pure . . . like you were brought up in a convent, or something.' She smiled gently at the irony of it.

There was a sudden hush in the crowd. Paul was speaking. Noreen was very conscious of him up on the platform, with Eileen there beside her. It made her uneasy, for she wondered if Eileen would somehow know what there was – unspoken – between them.

But Eileen was listening to what Paul said.

Each meeting ended like this, with an appeal to the crowd. Who would give their heart to Jesus? After all, they'd watched and listened, had their fun; now it was up to them to do something about it. No more sitting on the fence. They knew the facts now, and if they were going to go to the Devil, then they were going to go fully conscious.

Or put it another way. Jesus is asking you! He is calling to you, come to me, children! A new life will be yours. I love you. Come now, before it is too late . . .

The crowd dropped their eyes before Paul's. There was always this pause, this embarrassment. Who would be the first? A few shuffled about nervously. Then all eyes fixed upon the person who was brave enough, or guilty enough, or desperate enough, to make the move. The penitents walked up to where Paul, the leader, stood, and had gentle, joyful hands placed upon their heads. Often there were tears.

Now a stream of people would come up to the front, eager to drink of the promised cup, along with everyone else; eager to be good, to be received, to be loved. They offered up their hearts to Jesus, even if they weren't altogether sure what that meant. But they were sincere.

They only knew that here was hope of a purpose, meaning.

Take my life, come into my heart! I need you, I love you! It was an intoxication, a fever, which spread from one to another.

Life, heart, need, love, goodness: they would have laughed at these words before; now they were delirious with them. There was an opening, a flooding through – into what, they weren't quite sure; did it matter? The emotion and the passion were all. Here was truth, for they all felt it, together.

Eileen finished the ice-cream, shrugged and walked off, away from the crowd. Noreen felt compelled to follow her. It would be the hardest battle of her Christian life so far, for it was incumbent upon her to explain, to make Eileen see that the Catholic belief was misguided, that she was wrong, the Catholics were wrong. So God, or the born-again Christians, said. For the Catholic belief was not in the true Lord. Sure they didn't even know they would go to Heaven. They were not saved but damned. Their fate was not even uncertain but known already – to be born-again. For there is only one way, and few there are that find it. It happened to be the way that Noreen had found. God had chosen her, for some mysterious reason, through no virtue of her own. She was at pains to stress it.

Eileen listened quietly to what Noreen had to say.

They had gone down the steps on to the beach, by now almost deserted; evening was coming on, and people were going for their tea. There was only a man walking a dog, a rag of substance leaping after a stick at the edge of the great dun expanse. A woman bent down

140

for interesting bits left behind by the tourists. She picked up a cigarette end that was still glowing and stuck it hurriedly between her lips.

'You think that yours is the only way, don't you?' said Eileen suddenly, so that Noreen almost jumped. 'But why should your way be right, only yours, out of all the many ways that there are? Have you ever thought of that?'

'Because it says in the Bible . . .'

'Sure it was only men wrote that.'

The arguments. She had learnt them all – the stock replies. What were the answers?

'The men were inspired by God, Eileen.'

'Sure how do you know?'

Noreen had no answer; none of her own.

'Surely there are many different ways to reach God,' said Eileen. She hesitated. 'I would never be so – arrogant – as to believe that my way was the only way.'

Noreen's Da had said something like that once before. They watched in silence as a white-haired man, fine and muscly, ran into the pounding sea quite naked, oblivious of them. On the horizon the clouds were massed, like painted clouds, steel-grey and blue and turquoise, with ragged bright edges and the slowly dying amber sun piercing through.

'Don't think I hold it against you, Noreen,' said Eileen. 'Your religion, I mean. We're all entitled to our own opinion, aren't we? But don't force it on other people. It's not right, surely.'

All the training, the months of preparation, had turned dead on her. The worst thing was that deep down she agreed with Eileen. It must be the Devil speaking, urging the despicable notion of compromise upon her. She knew that there could be none.

Brendan found them on their way back. He was a big-built fellow, with shoulder-length fair hair that was cut straight across in a fringe at the front, and beneath it his eyes seemed to be always watching you, sly.

'Hiya Noreen!' He seemed uncommonly cheerful.

'Oh, hello.'

'I have a name, you know. It's Brendan.'

'I know.' She felt sullen with him. Unchristian.

He took Eileen's hand as they walked back. 'What's all this about religion, then?'

Noreen shrugged. She just wanted to be left alone. 'I've become a Christian, Brendan,' she said, with an effort. Of course, she should be showing him wonderful Christian love, turning the other cheek, as Jesus would have done – here was a test – but all she felt was this sullenness.

'Ach, Noreen! You ought to be careful, you know. A little religion's a dangerous thing. You'll end up a lonely ould woman, a burden to everyone, unless you marry some pious, impotent get.' He paused to light a cigarette, sheltering from the wind behind Eileen's back. 'Church twice on Sunday,' he went on, 'prayer meetings every evening, entertaining the vicar to tea in the afternoons.' He turned to Eileen to share the joke. 'She'll biblically accost every child in the neighbourhood – ould Noreen, the Bible machine, they'll call her!' His shoulders shook.

'Oh, for God's sake, Brendan, leave her alone!'

The Christian must be prepared to suffer for his (or, Noreen assumed, her) faith; when humiliated, she must turn the other cheek, as Jesus did; for Him, she must bear all things, as He bore all things for her.

Oh, but it was hard! Hard for Noreen, who still had a little human arrogance hidden in her soul.

She watched them go off hand in hand.

'See you, Noreen,' Eileen said over her shoulder.

'Oh, yes.'

Brendan put his hand on her backside, and she shook him off, laughing.

Noreen was left alone.

The sea was rushing in and sucking back again greedily, and Noreen's tears were salty too. Yet it was not for Eileen's lost soul that she wept, but for her own loss: that indefinable part of her which had surely gone with Eileen; and she wept for her own humiliation.

Paul bent his dark head in prayer for her. She must fight, fight, he exhorted her, win the battle against the Devil. For such a friendship, unblessed by God, could never be good anyway. There was no future in it, not with a Catholic, unless to lead her to the Lord. This was one of the crosses which Noreen must bear. Oh, God had prepared marvellous things for His child Noreen (he, Paul, knew); only for this reason did He lead her through darkness. 'For as the heavens are higher than the earth, so are my ways higher than your ways and my thoughts than your thoughts.' 'We cannot hope to understand His ways, His will,' said Paul. 'We must simply trust in the darkness.'

But aren't we just made blind? she wondered.

It was nearly over now. Tomorrow they would go up North again to jobs, schools, whatever: normality.

Before they went, they held a baptism in the sea for all the ones who had been saved through the mission. Paul stood out there in the water and plunged the people in. They wore old sheets or towels with their swimsuits underneath. They looked funny: women and children and men grinning in their bedclothes, as they waded into the ocean, where Paul dipped them and made them clean.

Noreen, still so young in the Lord, went too. The fellowship smiled and approved her. She had come home now; she had surely come home. She walked out through the creeping waves towards Paul, who seized her gently and dipped her towards the bottom of the world. It was like some wedding, only it was Christ she was marrying. All draped in virgin white, she walked out there and died, symbolically, to her old life, beneath the waves, then rose to a new one with Jesus. Paul's face was there, smiling. And then there was only Christ; Noreen had left herself beneath the waves.

She walked away from the camp that evening, when the beans and the prayers and the praising were over (they'd pray for her, otherwise). If only she could be a Christian alone. But the Bible, the fellowship, forbade it. It was too dangerous to be alone; there was strength in numbers. Otherwise, you'd slip away. But Noreen wanted her aloneness with the grass and the sky, with the silence of moving water, dark being. It was the only time when she could properly find herself and be strong; when she sensed a great, an immense God, quite different from the Saviour.

Noreen stood in silence, amongst stones and gorse. She watched a heron fly over, and she could hear the sound of dance music coming from the hall in the main street. Friday night – dance night; Eileen would be there, with Brendan. They too would be going back up North this weekend. As she stood listening to the faint strains of band music, it shamed her all of a sudden that their God, the Evangelical God, was too narrow for a generosity which would respect all humanity, as it danced, drank, prayed, loved, fought, died.

'Noreen!' Paul was coming through the field, until he stood beside her, touching her shoulder, his eyes questioning. 'All right?'

His voice was gentle. It was his gentleness which she loved; his darkness. A great dark gentle man, that was how he seemed to her.

'All right?' he repeated. He was worried for her.

She nodded. Paul could not see her face properly, for the sun had almost gone now. He did not question her further; he respected her quiet time alone with the Lord.

'Come on, then. It's late.' He led her back down the road towards the camp, where there was a small fire still burning. He was silent as they went, preoccupied with something. They stopped involuntarily just before the camp, in the gateway, from where you could see all the way down to the sea, even now: a dim, seething mass down there, a few lights swaying in the uneasy dusk; the smashing of dark pebbles in your ears. It seemed unreal, somehow, and yet more real than anything else.

'Noreen . . .' It was what she had known inside herself all along. Him, speaking her name like that. He spoke to her of love, the love of brother and sister in the Lord; and more – the love of man for woman in the Lord. Man for woman. She trembled. And yet hadn't she always known – always wanted – this? She seemed to watch from a great distance as her destiny fulfilled itself.

He kissed her – so tender – and they walked back to the camp hand in hand. The sky was cold and clear and full of stars. Noreen saw the future stretch before them, her and Paul; flattered in a way that it was she whom he had chosen, for she was considered so young yet, spiritually, and he so mature. She looked up to him, still: Paul, the leader. He knew so much, had already given so much, and she still had all to give (and yet hadn't she always recognized the old, or perhaps ageless, part of herself? What had always made her feel secretly special. And he could see it, too . . .).

There was no past now; only this future, which had always been waiting for her and Paul. She saw him: strong in faith and respected by all, he would head the fellowship and their Christian household. She saw him reading to the family from his large black Bible at night and firmly blessing their four children (yes, they would have four), patiently explaining points of doctrine to her, also his child. And she, fervent, strong in her own right, would support him, working at his side.

Perhaps they would be called to be missionaries in some far-off place, with the heat and flies and malaria; or perhaps their place was to stay in Northern Ireland, doing more mundane but, in the Lord's eyes, equally valuable things. They did not know yet. It did not matter. They would go wherever the Lord asked. They would share thoughts and prayers about God, fight battles together. Their children would wear jeans but clean shoes, attend prayer meetings, gently lead their schoolfriends to Christ. That was how it would be: a gentle, warm, loving life, working for the Lord . . .

It was late that evening when they finally sneaked into their separate tents. Noreen slept a strange half-sleep that night, her only consciousness being the sea, incessantly roaring and rushing and shattering in her ears. She was at peace. The battle with the Devil and Eileen was won.

9

Later, looking back on that Saturday afternoon in August, she could see all the omens of something dreadful about to happen; only at the time she was so preoccupied with her own struggles, she failed to see them.

There were the Black Marches in Armagh, as they drove through; the clouds gathering over the Dromara hills nearer home. Two seagulls blowing above her, mewing like lost kittens, as she walked down from the main road. Nessie staring at her from behind a cherished shrub at the new bungalow, then there were the cars in the drive. In the kitchen she could hear the cooker tick-ticking, and there was a fly buzzing over a pile of dirty dishes beside the sink.

The low murmuring in the good room, then the women staring at her in horror and pity. Isabel from the shop, with her great cow's eyes and lisp. They were all taking tea.

It was Big Iris who had taken control; she was the sort of woman who did.

'I came as soon as I heard,' she told Noreen. 'Your poor Ma . . . And we kept trying to reach you, love, but you'd already gone.'

Iris spoke to her in a loud whisper in the kitchen, and all the while Noreen kept looking at her and trying to work out why it was that she looked different. Something about her mouth; this trivial detail kept going through her mind, preventing her from concentrating properly on the thing that had happened.

'It's my teeth, love,' said Iris at last, not without a touch of pride. 'I've had new teeth.' And staring at Iris's large, shiny new teeth – then, it began to sink in.

The silly thing was that at first she thought it was her Ma who had had the accident. Your poor Ma, Iris kept saying. But it wasn't Ma. It was Da.

A bomb at the factory, which stood between the Protestant area and the big Catholic estate. The IRA had claimed responsibility. An accident – well, it wasn't him they'd meant to kill, specially; he was working overtime.

She couldn't grasp it at first. Ma sat in her bedroom staring at the window, dry eyed, pale, and Iris brought her cups of sweet tea. The doctor came and gave her tranquillizers, and after a bit she fell asleep on the made-up bed, with her dress all rumpled up round her legs. Noreen smoothed it for her.

Death. She couldn't believe in it . . . You never saw people go; they just went, and you thought there must be some mistake. She had seen the dog die, the first one they ever had. She'd named it Robbie. It chewed up Ma's shoes in its basket beneath the counter, and once it stole the Sunday roast. Ma had chased it out in a rage and wouldn't quit railing about it for ages after. But in the end she let it in again, for of course she'd an ould soft heart really; she'd big brown eyes herself, just like the dog's, and what else could you be, with eyes like that?

She remembered still the squeal of brakes, or of Robbie. It happened on her ninth birthday, after she'd opened her presents. The cards sat on the mantelpiece. He actually went flying up in the air like a doll, then papped down on the ground, with blood all dark and sticky looking beneath his head. Da had picked the poor thing up, and the head hung down all funny. Noreen was sick, and Da told her to get away inside.

She ran away in and sobbed into Ma, as if she were a wee girl again, and Ma could kiss and make it better. But the death-ache wouldn't go away; she was left with an awful emptiness and longing because the dog had gone. And all the time she was thinking that she must be able to do something to bring it back; the life couldn't disappear so easily, no. Then she'd looked up at Ma, and Ma's eyes were all wet. It was shocking. Not right that Ma should cry – Ma in her big apron that had a rhyme on and her warm, floured hands. But the tears were covering her blotchy face, shards of grief splintering Noreen. The dog was dead.

Now Granny Logan arrived and wept copiously. She took off her glasses to wipe her eyes, sniffing, and said, 'He's gone somewhere better, at least.'

Granda sat on the wee pouffe (he was far too big for it), with his knees pressed together, and silent tears streamed down his face like the rain streaming down the windows.

'All these things happen for a purpose,' Granny Logan went on. 'Though I can't understand it. Oh God, I can't!' She quietened. 'But God knows. We have to just accept it.'

Iris said that according to the ones who found him, he

just moved one knee, then lay still. He probably didn't suffer all that much.

It rained. That was the worst of it. Everything was so wet. Noreen walked about the fields, searching for him, for she hadn't found him in the coffin. There was only a body in there: a box of dead horror. What did that say of what a person had been? She saw his black hair fraying grey at the edges, and his face . . . grey too. She didn't know him.

'He's dead,' she said aloud, and the words fell flat. 'Da's dead.' (And it was all her fault, for all along she had thought that it was Ma she would have to take away with her.) Perhaps if she said the words enough, then she would begin to understand.

'Where are you?' She could hear herself, this voice, saying the words, and knew they were stupid, useless.

'Where are you, God?' the voice asked then.

Was Da in Heaven?

She didn't believe in Heaven.

And all the time the rain drizzled. At last she went back to the house. She had to admit that she hadn't found him.

Da. Desmond. Des. Where was he? It was all a mistake – for people had liked him OK. He was fond of a yarn, you know, with the neighbours in their gardens, or Isabel in the village shop, or just with the folks who walked the roads on Sunday afternoons and some fine evenings. He liked to be involved: giving out the books, reading at the Meeting, and last year they asked him to be Father Christmas for the Cubs. He was all chuffed. He was the sort who would always help you out, good for a bit of a crack, and respected in the Church. He was a gentle man, never tried to force anything on anybody; live and let live, he always said. Sure only recently he'd spoken to her of tolerance, generosity. It was all a mistake.

The only time, now, when she could picture him properly, was that time of the stealing. The very worst time. (Why not the good times? There must have been some.) That Monday evening when, at last, the knock came on her bedroom door. She remembered it: how she sat at the desk by the window, pretending to do her homework, but she was heaving inside. Here it was; she'd been waiting for it, of course, but now that it was actually here, she felt foolishly surprised.

He hitched up his dark trousers with the slim leather belt round the top, and cleared his throat.

'May I?' he said, in that polite way of his, and sat down on Noreen's white bedroom chair, awkward and out of place; a bit ridiculous altogether. He hadn't been in her bedroom for years, and didn't belong, with his hairy legs showing between the hitched-up trousers and patterned socks. He leaned forward, pressing his hands together between his knees, and cleared his throat again.

She had looked at him then, and it struck her for the first time that she didn't really know him at all; not inside. She remembered that realization so clearly; feeling rather surprised, in a way, that he should be her father. He had large blue eyes which Noreen didn't like looking into because of what she might find there. He'd look at her sometimes, and she'd look away. She couldn't remember how long it had been like that; maybe since she'd started at the grammar school, and so many things seemed different. She never went to the Meeting, nor to church, or at best she went in the morning now and then, just to keep the peace. He was disappointed, she knew, but he would never make her go. Her Da's Christianity was always a quiet, personal sort.

Whatever the reason, she didn't want to be close to him, and built a barrage of pleasantries, or unpleasantries, between them. She fended off his kisses before she could help herself. It made her feel bad, but still. It was most painless to remain on levels of tea and weather, like polite strangers, or school reports, where she usually did all right. That was the extent of their conversation and that was why this situation now, this facing one another, was so awful.

There had been better times, of course, but long ago. When she was wee, she would climb on to his lap when he came in from his work. It felt safe there. He would slump in an armchair in front of the tele and go all soft and loose. She would put her head under his chin, which was all rough at the end of the day, even though he'd shaved that morning. She used to see him in front of the bathroom mirror, covered in foam, and later sticking plaster on his face where he'd cut himself.

She remembered walking with him on dusky evenings, with the dark trees murmuring to the stream and the bushes full of secrets. She held his hand. Then tramping back up the moonfields into the mundane house, where the flickering tongues of flame nuzzled the hearth, poor reflections of the warm heart of earth. Things – togetherness – which she couldn't bear later; rare occasions when she had felt able to admit something – love? – for him, but in secret. Not that Da was the sort to talk much, really talk, but Noreen sensed that he would have shown his world to her, if she had let him. Yet she could not. His bared soul would have embarrassed her with its nakedness.

And there was Da going on about the stealing and trying to find out the reason for it. As if there was a reason. Did they not give her enough money? he asked. They wouldn't have her wanting for anything, she knew that. Yes, yes. Noreen almost wished that he would lose his temper, yell at her, be angry and even unreasonable; it would have made her feel better, somehow. But he went through this thing of quietly treating her as a sensible, grown-up person, and it filled her with rage and guilt.

He no longer appealed to her Christianity, to her love for the Saviour, for he knew that she did not have any. He never mentioned it, but she knew he prayed for her; and for Ma, who did not have his inner fire. He was so alone with his Christianity.

How hurt Ma was, he had said. He sighed, suddenly looked old and tired, sitting there on Noreen's white bedroom chair. He knew that he no longer had power over her, perhaps that she did not respect him as she should (and yet she did not know why). He surely knew, and was weak, and could have cried with his helplessness, because of her lack of love. Noreen saw herself in him, then; they shared the same eyes, the curve of the cheek, even the shape of a lip. It filled her suddenly with a compassion for him, an unutterable tenderness, and yet she could say nothing.

It seemed to her now that he left again, shutting the door quietly behind him. Again she turned out the lamp and lay on the bed in darkness, apart from the moon which tore through the flimsy curtains and shivered on the floor. He was gone. She slept.

She woke in the night and got up. The house was quiet. She entered the rooms where he had been, switching on the lights so that the cats blinked and stretched. His chair swung mockingly empty by the unmade fire, his boots ached on the cold hearth. His clothes sprawled on the bed, hung uselessly on the arms of chairs, waited in cupboards. It was hopeless.

She knew then that she wouldn't find him here, either; not whole. There was so much of a person. How could you begin to clear him away? It was this that pained her most. Those men that killed him didn't know, didn't care; they saw only what they killed him for, just that one thing (and they thought that gave them the right . . .). They didn't realize that Noreen would be picking up bits of him for the rest of her life.

In school the headmaster expressed his condolences during Assembly; schoolfriends squeezed her arm. There was the funeral to get through: so many people Da had known; the tea to give afterwards. And then all that was over. It was the first 'normal' day – if there ever could be a normal day again. There had been people every day until now, and legal things to sort out, which left Ma confused and exhausted. Today there was nothing. She had got up and pottered about the house. She went outside, then came back in and sat looking at Da's chair by the fireplace. Noreen made the lunch, which Ma pushed about with her fork and then left on the plate. Noreen threw the congealed mess away afterwards and washed up. She brought Ma her tablets with a glass of water, and Ma had a sleep on the bed. She came back through at about half past three, still in her quilted dressing-gown, her hair dishevelled. She looked old, Noreen thought. Her face was wan without the make-up which she wore for work, and there were dark shadows under her eyes. Grey was showing through her brown hair, which she hadn't bothered to tint recently. Noreen put the kettle on. She had just set out the cups and wet the tea, when she heard the squeak of the garden gate.

'Oh no,' said Ma. She pulled at her dressing-gown in a distracted sort of way. 'Not now.'

Noreen glanced at her nervously. The doorbell rang. There was a silence. Then Ma sighed. She seemed to pull herself together slightly.

'See who it is then, Noreen,' she said, resigned. 'Go on.'

Noreen opened the door, and there was Eileen. Beside her on the step stood Mrs McAllister, looking a bit self-conscious in a dark dress and high-heeled shoes. She thrust a paper package at Noreen.

'Just a wee something to help yous out,' she said. 'Sure your Ma would hardly be feeling like baking.'

Noreen could feel the slight warmth of the wheaten bread through the paper. She mumbled her thanks. Eileen and Mrs McAllister were still standing there expectantly. Eileen wore a skirt and blouse, but Noreen could see that she was still tanned from the weeks down South. Her bare neck was freckled.

'Come in,' Noreen said then. 'You'd better come in and have some tea.' She stood back and opened the door wide for them.

Ma looked startled as Noreen showed them into the sitting-room. 'How good of you,' she murmured. She put a hand to the buttons of her dressing-gown. 'You must excuse –'

'Not at all, not at all, dear,' said Mrs McAllister hurriedly. 'We quite understand . . .'

'Will you sit down?' asked Noreen, motioning to the settee. They did so, awkwardly. Eileen perched on the edge of her cushion, but Mrs McAllister occupied all of hers, clutching her tan handbag on her knee. Noreen sat down on a chair beside them. Ma was on her chair by the window.

Noreen cleared her throat. 'And how's Geraldine?' she asked, to break the silence which had fallen.

'Oh, grand, grand,' replied Mrs McAllister enthusiastically. She crossed her legs at the ankles, then uncrossed them again.

'And Michael?'

'He's grand too, thanks, Noreen.'

There was another silence. Mrs McAllister patted her hair.

Ma spoke. 'I suppose you've finished school now, Eileen. Or will you be going on studying?'

'Oh no,' said Eileen. 'I'm all finished wi' that now.' She was proud. 'Sure I have a job as a cashier down the town. In Willis's,' she added. 'Starting next week.'

It was then that Ma noticed the ring on Eileen's finger. 'Lord save us! And how long has this been going on?'

Eileen blushed. She and Brendan had become engaged when they were on holiday down South. He had proposed on their last evening.

'And when will the big day be?'

It would be next summer, soon after her eighteenth birthday. Now that she and Brendan had made up their minds, they wanted to wait as little as possible. Mrs McAllister shook her head, smiling.

'Let's see the ring, then,' said Ma.

Eileen put forward her finger, where the three diamonds nestled proudly, and Ma admired it. 'Look, Noreen, isn't it lovely?' Noreen grunted. She got up and made herself busy getting the tea. After a minute Eileen followed her out to the kitchen. Noreen looked round. Eileen stood by the counter, hands clasped together in front of her. She cleared her throat.

'I'm sorry, Noreen,' she said then.

Noreen nodded.

'I'm sorry,' repeated Eileen. There was nothing else to say.

Noreen stirred the tea and poured the milk into the cups. Her hand shook slightly and she spilt a bit. Eileen took a cloth and wiped it up. They took the cups into the sitting-room.

'A shocking thing,' Mrs McAllister was saying. She was leaning forward in her seat. She shook her head. 'A shocking, dreadful thing.' Then the big woman reached over for Ma's hand and squeezed it briefly. She dropped it again hurriedly and took the tea which Noreen was holding out to her.

Ma was looking down at her hand. Noreen stood before her.

'Your tea,' she said.

Ma took the cup wordlessly. Noreen saw that there were tears in her eyes.

*

A few days later Noreen found the time to go into town and buy Eileen a wee silver tray for an engagement present. She sent it in the post. The same afternoon she told Ma about Paul. She hadn't wanted to break the news sooner, but now, she felt, the time was right. Ma became all flustered, put a hand to her face and smiled. Then the smile faded.

'If only your Da . . .'

They invited Paul to tea one Sunday afternoon – he in his suit, they in their best dresses. Ma was flattered by him. How could she not be? He with his tall figure and dark hair, gentle voice and manners. He discussed books with her, not religion. She was overwhelmingly relieved.

They came to rely on him rather – the man of the house. He was a tower of strength and prayer, of course. He called often – you could hear the whine of the wee motorbike coming down the road – to make sure that they were both coping, and that Ma was not too depressed with the tranquillizers. He helped them too with certain legal matters, which they did not know how to deal with. He was everything he should be.

Noreen did not go to the meetings – and he understood – nor did they go to church; Ma said she could not stand it yet, all the faces, but she took to saying Grace before meals, just as he used to.

She was back at work now, but would sit, vacant, for half an hour at a time. She wept, and it was Noreen's job to comfort her, which she did gladly, for it stopped her from thinking too much about it herself. She worked like a demon in school. Ma said she must get her exams; he would have wanted her to do well. Now that he was not there, they were at pains to do everything he wanted.

She still ought to go away to university, said Ma, like she'd planned; he had always wanted only the best for her.

Noreen was shocked. She had forgotten all about that.

The forms had come back – but she'd filled those in so long ago, in another world, before Paul, before Da.

'But you'd be all alone,' she said.

'Oh, I'd be all right. Don't you bother your head about me. Ach, it'll get better. And you'd come back, sometimes, wouldn't you?'

'Of course, of course I'd come back.' But it wasn't even in their plan for her to go away anywhere – hers and Paul's.

If only the days weren't so long, Ma complained. Or not so much the days but the evenings. Not that they would have talked much: he would have read the paper, she would have done her knitting, watched the TV. It was just having him there.

It took a long time. A long, long time. Another summer was over. Winter was on them again: the bare days, when the sun went early, at four o'clock, closing you into your house with the night, or leaving you to fumble your way in a cold, dark world that was lit only by the faint, isolated stars of windows. And the mornings, still night, dragging on your clothes and eating a slow breakfast, shivering to school just as it was getting light. It was right for their time of sadness, the dark without mirroring their dark within. You flickered through days that were pale and brittle as eggshells. It was hard to remember that there ever had been a summer: the vividness of its colour, the quality of its light, the bands and holidays and ice-cream, the sea salt in tangled hair. It seemed that the world had always been like this – always winter.

In the spring Paul pressed Noreen to come down to Belfast and choose a ring, make it all official, but for some reason, faced with his earnestness, his quivering nose, she hesitated. She was not quite ready yet, she said; he must give her a little more time. He nodded, disappointed, but understanding. They couldn't wait for ever, though.

She received a card from Eileen, thanking her for the tray and inviting her to go round and see the presents; it was customary to invite all the people who had given. Noreen immediately regretted the silver tray. She didn't want to go, sure she wouldn't know anybody, but Ma said that she ought to go, if only for a short while. It was only polite. You had to observe these traditions, didn't you? They gave a sense of continuity, of dignity, even, to the whole cycle, birth, marriage, death. And Eileen did used to be her best friend, after all.

It was a Wednesday evening when she walked by the IRA scrawled in the road and swung open the lilac gate. The sitting-room was full of women gossiping over tea. They all touched and admired the engagement ring with its three diamonds – and the presents! There were such a lot. Eileen McAllister had done well for herself. There were glasses and plates and bowls, even a complete dinner service – the willow pattern, which Eileen had always liked. Someone had given a pretty kettle with flowers on it, someone else a set of kitchen knives. There were sheets, pillowcases and one of those continental quilts; two vases, an iron and even a coffee machine. She'd done well, had Eileen. People had been generous:

friends, neighbours, relatives, the girls in work. They all wanted to give some wee thing to see the young couple off to a good start. It was only once in a lifetime after all.

Eileen was in her element. The presents were all laid out, with their paper, on her pink eiderdown; the gift tags neatly arranged alongside, so that everyone could see who had given what. The women admired and sighed, and told Eileen what a lovely bride she'd be, all dressed in white. It was the greatest day in any girl's life. She must be so excited! Eileen, wearing her flowered dress and diamond ring, blushed and smiled and said yes.

Where would they be living, then? Did they have a house? It was ever so expensive, nowadays, buying your own place. So hard for the young ones just starting out.

Yes, Eileen said modestly, they'd managed a very small flat above a shop in Church Street. It would be handy for work and all. Yes, Brendan had a job in the new car factory. They'd both saved hard, her and him, out of their wages, and their parents had helped them out a bit. The flat would do fine for just the two of them . . .

Then the women smiled and wagged their fingers. Not two for long, though!

And Eileen blushed some more.

Noreen made herself busy, handing out tea and scones, even answering the door to people. The women glanced at her covertly.

'Poor child,' she heard one say.

Mrs McAllister put her large red hands on Noreen's shoulders. There was such a lot to do! she told them all. She'd hardly realized before, but then her own wedding had never been such a grand affair. It was what Eileen wanted, though! There was just so much to organize, what with the invitations, the dresses, the cake, the wedding breakfast . . . Well, of course, they knew it all for themselves.

But the women smiled tolerantly and made believe it was the first time. You were bound to be excited, when your daughter was to be married, especially when it was the youngest, somehow: happy, and sad. But you soon forgot the grief.

Mrs McAllister couldn't believe that.

'At least she'll not be too far away, though,' she said, wiping her cheek. 'You wouldn't leave your ould mother altogether, would you, Eileen?'

'Sure I'm only going three mile down the road!' said Eileen, a bit impatient.

'Oh, you'll understand one day, though,' sniffed Mrs McAllister, 'When you've a daughter of your own.'

'And what about Noreen?' someone said, inevitably. It was the same woman who had said 'Poor child' in that way; Mrs Murphy lived two along from the McAllisters, a small, fragile-looking woman with a worn face. Her venetian blind always moved slightly as Noreen went by to call for Eileen, or the two walked by arm in arm.

Now all eyes turned on Noreen – legitimately, at last.

'You'll be the next to go, I don't doubt!'

Then it was Noreen's turn to blush, and mumble that she didn't have it in mind just yet. She didn't want them to know; she was glad that she had no ring. She'd like to see round her a bit, first, she told them.

'Oh, aye, indeed. You're just right,' said another of them, with a Belfast accent. 'Sure you've plenty of time yet. See a bit of the world first.' And then the two of them turned away, disapproving, and not without a little pity.

'Noreen's going to study, you know,' Mrs McAllister told them. 'She's going to university over the water . . . aren't you, Noreen?'

'Well, I've not decided yet . . .'

'Are you, now? Still studying, then – at your age?'

'And what're you going over the water for? Is Northern Ireland not good enough for you?'

'Ach, well . . . she'll maybe meet some nice fellow over there.'

'The poor mother,' said someone else. 'D'you not think of your mother, child?'

The mother. So alone.

'And what d'you think of it, Eileen? Your friend going off and leaving you?'

Eileen had shrugged. 'Some are just happy where they're born,' she said simply, 'and some just aren't.'

'Sure she'll not be worried now – sure she'll be married.'

Noreen started handing round a new plate of scones which Mrs McAllister brought in from the kitchen. She stayed afterwards to help clear up all the mess, but she was glad when the last of the women were away and she could go home.

10

They started in May, the first exams: three, sometimes four a week. Noreen didn't go to bed until the small hours, and then was up again at half-past five, reading and muttering to herself on the bedroom floor. Ma scolded and said it couldn't be good for her; she ought to just get a good night's sleep. But Noreen worked as if she had a demon in her, until at last, in June, it was all over.

Then there was a rare sort of freedom. There were no classes, though it wasn't yet the end of the term, and people turned up in school just for the crack, dressed in their everyday clothes, and all the girls made up. They ran off round the shops and cafés, and some of them went into the pub at lunchtime, to drink beer and play cards. Noreen saw them come lurching out sometimes, in the late afternoon, as she walked by with Paul. It made her feel cross, somehow, to see them. She held Paul's hand tight.

Oh, she wanted to live for God. She did. She had seen the truth of Him. But there was a devil in her too, that old feeling of wildness, which had always been there, always, though it was well hidden. She must experience everything, she felt, everything: good, bad, love, hate, pleasure, pain. For only by knowing all of these things would she understand any of them.

She allowed Paul to take her into Belfast and buy her a solitaire diamond ring. She looked at the dainty thing on her finger and slipped it on and off over her knuckle until Paul told her to be careful with it, or she would lose it, and them not yet one day engaged! They had lunch in a posh restaurant in Belfast, where white-jacketed waiters bent from the waist to show a discreet bottle of wine. Yes, they had wine, to mark the occasion, and a wonderful chicken flambéed in brandy. They held hands across the table, discussing their future – the great wedding – and eating each other's ice-cream.

The step was taken. She felt as though her life were back on course again, with Paul, the husband, God, the Father. It was right.

Noreen was light-headed as she took the bus home, and it was an effort to walk down the lane, though she seemed to get there quick. Ma laughed with delight at the ring.

'At last!' she said, thankfully. 'At last. Oh, it's great, Noreen.'

Noreen knew that it was what Ma wanted, despite talk of going away, 'the best'; she wanted her son-in-law and Sunday visits and wee grandchildren to bounce on her knee. It was what a part of Noreen wanted too, and she thought that such an existence – the shopping, and the gossip, the children, him coming home at six o'clock, the supper on the table – it could make her happy; content, at least. Her dream to travel – oh, it was only a dream.

Once, when she was seven, she had gone with Ma to see the sister who lived over the water in London.

They took the night ferry to Liverpool, and for the first time she felt the strangeness of heading for the open sea in a large boat full of unknown people. They were travellers now, suspended in time and space, it seemed, neither here nor there. No stops. Just rocking in a dark limbo. The water was dark and rushing, and as the Belfast lights slowly faded into obscurity, she was suddenly gripped by panic. It was the only world she knew. She didn't want to leave. But it was too late. The city went, and only the wind and seagulls were left, washing with the water. The boat was taking her, and she was filled with this aching strangeness.

They had gone into the lounge-bar, which was large and crowded, impersonal with bright lights and plastic seats. Here groups of men blubbered and told bleary jokes. Children girned, and tired-looking women drank vodka. Ma let Noreen have a few sips of sweet sherry to help with the sea-sickness. They sat beside a woman with washed-out eyes who poured out her life to them: the husband who beat her, the son out of work, the daughter with child – without man – and the burning out. Ma made clucking noises in her throat and shared a little vodka with the woman, until finally she dozed off, with her mouth open, and Ma took Noreen away down into their narrow cabin. They shared it with two other women who were already in bed. You could see them lumped beneath the rough covers, one with a long grey plait hanging down her back.

Noreen slept in the top bunk with her face close to the ceiling, and all night long it seemed that she lay awake in the close dark, with the boat groaning and swaying. She liked it. Then she must have fallen asleep, because the next thing she knew, there was a great banging on their door, and then the next one, and so on all along the passage. If you went first class, then they brought you tea and toast in the morning, but going second you just got this rude banging at six o'clock.

After breakfast in the cafeteria they waited in a great crowd with all the others for the ferry finally to touch the dock and the doors to open. It happened at last, with much shouting and bumping, and they all streamed down the gangway into the grey dawn. Then there was another long wait while they were all searched and had their identification checked by weary men in uniform.

A bus took them to the railway station, and it was strange to see the early morning streets filling with postmen and milk vans and people on their way to work, dressed in suits, or raincoats and high heels. They all seemed swift and purposeful, whether they were crossing roads or buying papers or waiting in queues for buses, and Noreen could not get used to the idea that this was their home, which for her was a disturbing adventure.

The train journey was uneventful, but then, when they reached London and Ma's sister Carol met them, there was the tube: the Underground. She hated that: the hot, artificial wind that blew up the tunnels; the sudden rush of the train arriving; the surge of people getting on and off. Then the awful journey in the airless compartment, for the train was packed right to the doors, squeezing the breath from her. She clung on to a railing beside Carol, who was busy talking away to Ma, and stared into the outer darkness which was splattered yellow with the occasional neon lights of stations.

Yet afterwards she would sometimes yearn for the rush of waves in darkness, the sudden splash of unknown lights, the people at home in unfamiliar places. The anticipation of these things would fill her with pain.

She took driving lessons that summer. She got her test in July, and then she took Ma away to windy beaches and for wet walks in the Forest Park. She drove the beige car which Da had swopped for the red one, and tried to clean it once a fortnight.

Ma cooked fish for tea in the evenings, or sometimes they had quiche from the new delicatessen, or brown rice with vegetables. Not so much meat now that Da wasn't there. But they still said Grace and went to church on Sundays. Ma liked the walk and she enjoyed the hymns, especially at the festive times, like Christmas and Easter.

Now and then they even went together to the concerts in Belfast. Noreen sped them down the motorway towards the lights of Belfast which you could see all spread out, and Ma worried that the police would get her, for she still had her 'R' plates. But Noreen laughed and patted her arm reassuringly, so that Ma worried instead about her not having both hands on the wheel.

The concerts were great – a bit of sophistication, at last – with everyone all dressed up and chattering, then the hush and the trembling violin in the semi-dark. Another time there were Viennese waltzes; Ma's head moved about from side to side, and her eyes were moist when all the people began clapping.

Afterwards they went into the new French restaurant for a treat; it was jam-packed at ten o'clock, but they managed to find a seat. They had a glass of wine each, 'crêpes' with ratatouille in, and afterwards profiteroles. It was great.

They passed close to Paul's flat on the way home, up the avenue where the flowering chestnut trees were, and the row of old red brick houses. She looked, but there were no lights – it was gone eleven o'clock. She could see a light at the top of another house, and several people inside – you could just see their heads moving about. She wondered about them as she lay in bed that night: who they were, what they were doing, what their names were. What did they talk about? They'd be students, of course; students. The dark figures caught in the bare light of an unknown house filled her with wistfulness.

A stiff white envelope arrived in the post for Noreen. It was the invitation to Eileen's wedding. A white card with gold lettering.

It was all a matter of form, her invitation. She realized that.

She propped it up on the mantelpiece behind the carriage clock in the good room, and stared at it for a long time.

Eileen's wedding was four weeks away. Four weeks.

MR AND MRS D. R. McALLISTER

*request the pleasure of
the company of*

———

Miss Noreen Logan

———

at the marriage of their daughter,

*EILEEN MARY,
with MR BRENDAN McVEIGH*

*at St. Anne's on Saturday,
28th August at 3.30 pm
and afterwards at St. James' Hall.*

———

RSVP

The formal card made it seem more definite, inevitable –
the end of something. And a beginning, she supposed;
of what, she was not sure. Everything was changing;
they were all moving on. It made her uneasy.

Paul was organizing school trips in the Mournes that
summer. She didn't see much of him. Ma was working.
She spent most of the time alone. It was like wandering
through that tenth summer again. The summer of leav-

ing village school, of invoking the Spirit, of waiting for change – what she thought of as the 'Summer of the Glass'.

The fields were golden again, the house a dark, cool oasis in the middle of a burning stubble-desert. The evenings were warm and balmy, heady with the scent of new cut grass, hazy with seeds and rags of flowers. Noreen swam in them. Green turned golden overnight, and the afternoons stretched on for ever, dreaming into drowsy evening that turned again into morning. It was as though all the summers of her life were being concentrated into this one: the summers of running the countryside with Eileen, those summers of lying together in saffron hayfields, eyeing Thomas who worked the next field. She remembered him then, adolescent; how he was tall and lean, with dark hair and a pale, freckled skin that burned red beneath the sun and their own furtive glances.

She wandered through the cottage where they'd once played, all dark insides and silent stone, only the hum of Ma's vacuum cleaner somewhere far off. How blissfully quiet it always was, and the ceilings bulged like a pregnant woman's early belly, stirring their imaginations. They played hide-and-seek and huddled together in the clothes press, close in a womb of warm, dark companionship, sharing secrets, while the cistern gurgled and rumbled.

She roamed about the old places, trying to pin everything – oh, everything – in her mind. She wandered about the town, looking in the shop windows, past the boot boys who swung their faded legs on the wall, gazing at the soldiers who grinned at her. She stared in at McCauley's window, where the girls shovelled up the iced buns and doughnuts and wrapped warm wheaten bread.

They were building a new roundabout down the bottom of Bridge Street, and a vast new health centre nearby, all of four storeys high. She went into McCauley's and took a cup of tea, for old times' sake. Some boot boys were sprawled in a corner, drinking Coke, and there was coffee spilt on the floor. Outside an armoured car rumbled by, bristling with guns; you could see the checkpoint, and some barbed wire above the wall opposite, which was painted with some slogan. An old man tramped by, wearing a raincoat and a placard which said, 'The end of the world is nigh'.

Paul came home, and his eyes shone as he kissed her. She felt glad of him all of a sudden; glad of his strength and joy, his companionship. She found herself thinking of their life together again; of its warmth, its safety. The children they would have, the sharing, the Sunday meals together. He would become a Head of Department, and she would even take a wee job somewhere for a bit of extra cash. She clung to him, so that he laughed.

He came every day now to take her out. Sometimes they went away to the mountains or to the sea, but mostly Noreen preferred the familiar walks around the lough, where she and Eileen used to run. The scrubby fields and crumbling stone walls tore at her throat with memories. Oh, it was here that they ran – here, in this country of seeping bogs and pert drumlins, where sheep inhabited ruins of cottages and wrinkled herons grew from stones, fossilized myths. The country that rocked her in its bosom, dark and sweet, just her, the gods, and Eileen. If only she could grasp it all again . . .

Paul's tanned arm was around her, comforting, but she simply wiped the tears, and could not explain. He wanted to pray with her. She could not. She could sense that he was becoming impatient. But she found prayer hard now, since Da went. It was almost as if he had taken God with him. She had no spiritual life. She must simply wait, Paul said. It would get better. Trust God – He would not abandon her in her time of need. She saw his absolute sincerity, his conviction, and wished that she could give herself so completely. She wished that she had more – more steadiness, perhaps.

At home they looked together at the early engagement presents which Noreen had set up on the sideboard in the good room: some hall-marked cutlery from Ma, a silver tray and silver servers from the women in her office, a crystal glass dish from Mrs Baird along the way. Paul's parents had given a china teapot with cups and saucers; the rest of the set would be for the big present. Mrs Megarry had wept and hugged Noreen to her, when the news was broken; Mr Megarry had shaken her hand in his gruff way and called upon the Lord to bless them. Matrimony was a holy undertaking, he told them; a good marriage was heaven on earth, patting his wife's hand, so that she looked down and blushed.

Noreen didn't know why it was that she had felt like some sort of a fraud that night, sitting at the long dinner table with the Megarrys.

Paul was telling her about the meeting on Saturday night. It was to be a great night, for the famous American evangelist was returning. The door-to-door work had been successful, many people had promised to come; the Lord was moving. He wanted Noreen to be there. He had been patient so far; but it was time that she tried, at least.

She hesitated, then promised. The time had come, she realized, to get down off the fence, as Paul had once said. She did want to please; to do right. She would go. But then she suddenly remembered.

'It's the wedding . . .'

There was a silence.

'Whose wedding?' Paul picked up Eileen's wedding invitation from the mantelpiece. He read from it. 'The marriage of – Eileen Mary. Isn't that your Catholic girl?'

'Aye.'

She played with the signet ring on her finger. AL it was inscribed. Ma had given it to her lately, amongst other bits of jewellery, which she wanted her to have (almost as if she thought she was going to die too, or something).

Paul replaced the invitation behind the clock. 'Well, I don't suppose you'll be going to it.'

'Why not? We used to be best friends, you know.'

Things were different now, of course: different lives, as Eileen had once said. But she would go to the wedding, if only to mark an ending, to formalize what had been and now was gone. Yet, even now, with Da's death and Eileen's marriage, she was becoming precariously aware of the tender beginnings of something else; a new sympathy in the rare meeting of their eyes over stained teacups.

'She's a Catholic, though,' said Paul, surprised. 'I mean . . . it's a union which would never be blessed by the Lord, Noreen. I don't think you should go,' he said firmly. 'It wouldn't be right.'

For a brief moment she glimpsed what marriage to Paul would be like: the moralizing, the fastidiousness, the gradual suffocation.

'Sure I've accepted already,' Noreen told him. 'It's all fixed.'

There was a silence in the room. She had the impression that Paul was somehow swelling, swelling. But his voice was controlled, quiet, even cold. He had never spoken to her like this before. It chilled her.

'How can there be a choice, Noreen? Between God . . . and the Devil . . .'

She said nothing. Suddenly it was important, very important, that she go to this wedding.

'I'll leave you to think it over,' he said shortly. 'I've to be in Belfast by seven.' He glanced at his watch, picked up his jacket. He didn't touch her as he left; just said, 'Pray, Noreen.'

The door slammed, and the house shuddered again into quietness. Noreen remained sitting on the sofa, staring into the dregs of coffee which stained the china cups on the polished round table, where once she raised spirits with Eileen.

She'd always suspected this about herself. She recalled that analogy which once had given her so much pleasure: the born-again analogy. Well, the long pregnancy was over now, but the child wasn't the one which people had expected. She had made God and Paul go off in disgust.

His face had on it a look – she had seen it before somewhere. Then it came to her – how he once told Johnnie Reilly that he must no longer pray to statues, and his eyes – those blue eyes pierced with a hardness – it made you shudder. She had seen it on certain festive days – the Orangemen, the anniversary marchers, the ones with a burning cause. They saw only one thing, those ones, and they murdered men like her Da.

She remembered how, when she was wee, she used to challenge God sometimes, to try and prove that He existed. For she wanted Him to exist. She would put a button, or some similar object, in a certain place before she went to bed at night, and she would say, now if it's moved in the morning, I'll believe in God. Of course, it never worked, because you had to believe first. God's terms, not yours.

Then you saw other people believing – so bright and sure! – and you wanted to believe too. And then it seemed that all sorts of things happened, and you believed all the more that you were right. It was so easy to fit what happened into the framework of your belief; so easy, when you had all those people together, believing in the same thing. You thought you saw everything – but really you saw nothing.

No surrender! you shouted. No compromise! For you were right. You couldn't give an inch to anyone else's point of view; you had to be strong, stick out for your way, the best, the only way. And then you, the great love-person, the visionary, the saviour of the world – it happened gradually; you didn't realize – you couldn't see your love for people any more, only causes and battles and slogans, rights and wrongs; the people lost their faces. And he, the moderate, the live and let live man – oh, of course he'd had his faults, he was human – whom she'd never been able to love enough: oh God, he'd died for it.

If only she could tell him; she wanted to go home and tell him. You know that voice – the one I thought belonged to Jesus? Well, all along it was just dry autumn leaves rustling in the wind.

A lonely thing.

11

And then, all too soon, it was there. It was Eileen McAllister's wedding day – a windy Saturday in August; mercifully, the sun shone (or had Eileen arranged that too, along with the hair appointments and the dress alterations, the taxis and the flowers and the ushers?).

Mrs McAllister wore pink and smiled at the front of the church. Even her shoes and hat were pink, and she had a little pink veil to cover her face. She smiled behind it. She was proud of Eileen. They had done it: this was the day.

Brendan wore tails and a red face. He couldn't look at anyone without blushing. You could see the back of his neck, all bare and vulnerable, for he'd just had his hair cut in honour of the occasion. He caught Noreen's eye once and grimaced, and she smiled back. She wouldn't hold anything against him, and he didn't want bad feeling, not on his wedding day.

Eileen was beaming and radiant in her white, as a young bride should be. Her red hair was pinned up, and you could see her lovely neck, creamy and smooth. She held her father's arm lightly and looked straight ahead of her, up the church to where the priest waited.

The heads all turned to watch the bridal party as they trembled up the aisle. Hatted heads and bald heads and hairy heads. The carnations, whites and pinks, stared

179

from suits and dresses. Noreen wondered what it must be like to be Eileen. Oh, it was a long way. They went so slowly. Right at the top you could see the priest, robed, hands clasped, like some monarch or god waiting to receive them. Somewhere nearby, rigid, was Brendan, who looked like a frog somehow in his tails.

And then they had made it. Eileen was doing her kneeling bit, and the priest's voice going on about loving and caring and obeying. Eileen was promising to obey Brendan for ever.

Noreen was thinking about leaving. Soon. Her mother's back curved beneath the old lamb's-wool cardigan. She'd broken a dish. Noreen thought that nothing would ever hurt so much again.

'Well, have yous set the day?' Ma had asked.

'No,' said Noreen. 'No. Ma – it's over. All that's over.'

'Oh.' Ma was subdued. Examined her nails. No wee grandchildren. No Sunday afternoons together. 'Oh,' she said.

Noreen stole a glance at her. Agnes, Ma, with her brown eyes and country face, freckles and a bump on her nose, high brows. She was a bit plump and had a way of rounding her shoulders beneath her cardigan . . . It filled Noreen with a pang of love, which was out of proportion to the situation. Noreen had now and then hugged Ma like she felt, and Ma had laughed, surprised, then told her to get away on, for she'd her work to be doing.

They weren't suited, her and Paul; they just weren't suited, she told Ma, who nodded. They sent back the presents with short notes of explanation. A formal exchange of letters with Paul. She was sorry; he understood that she had changed, that their relationship was no longer blessed.

A few loose ends tied up, yet so much still unfinished – like with her Da. If only there could be a trailing off, a proper ending, it might be easier to bear. But it never was like that. There was only a cutting off, abrupt; you never had finished. And life – some life – went on.

She'd missed the nuptial mass somehow. Now the rings were being exchanged. The music was playing. Everyone was smiling. There was the signing of the book out of sight somewhere, and then the long journey back down the aisle. But the crucial bit was over. They had all said their lines okay, and no one had tripped up. Eileen walked on Brendan's arm now, instead of her father's. Mr McAllister had given his daughter to Brendan McVeigh. Cameras and faces flashed at them, and they all smiled.

Outside, the wind heaved the dresses round the girls' legs, and you could see Eileen's frilly garter. There were two bridesmaids, both in pink: Geraldine, and Brendan's sister, Siobhan, who was fair-haired like him, with a big nose. They were photographed on the steps, in the doorway, then out across the grass, from where you could see the lough lying in green fields and reeds, and, nearby, the tall walls of the Forest Park.

Then the cars whisked them away, Eileen and Brendan first, drowning in confetti. You could see their glowing faces waving in the back; even Brendan was happy, now that the worst was over. Noreen was squeezed into a car with Mr and Mrs McAllister and the flower girl, who poked her feet into Noreen's dress.

At the reception the bridal party all stood in a line in the hallway, greeting the guests as they came in, with handshakes and kisses. Brendan offered his hand to Noreen. 'No hard feelings, eh, Noreen?' She shook her head and took his outstretched hand. Eileen was flushed with excitement and laughing as she held Noreen's hand, then it was on to the next.

The tables were all laid out ready in the long hall, posh in their stiff white tablecloths. Noreen had a place just below the bridal table, which was raised up and faced everyone else, as if it were the stage for a play. There was soup and turkey and vegetables and ice-cream, or you could have fruit salad if you wanted. They had orange juice to drink. The flower girl had Coca-Cola and spilt it all down Eileen's Auntie's best dress.

Brendan and Eileen sat together, in between the parents and bridesmaids and best man. It was allowed now, for them to sit together. They were man and wife. Everyone kept staring at them.

'What a lovely bride she is!' they said.

Or, 'What a lovely couple they make!'

Noreen wondered what it was like to go for a honeymoon. Eileen and Brendan were going to Jersey – and managing a washing machine.

Eileen sat there in her veiled white and glowed at everyone. Noreen tried to think of other things. She looked at Brendan, who looked far too young all of a sudden, sitting there in his white shirt and black tails and short hair – like some kid playing at dressing up.

They cut the cake together, Brendan and Eileen, and

the cameras clicked again. There was champagne, and the guests toasted the newly-weds, then the brides-maids, who blushed, and Mr and Mrs McAllister. There were awkward speeches and the inevitable awful jokes. Noreen fidgeted with her paper napkin, which had some strange floral design on it.

Then, after the reception, it was time for the dance. It was gone six o'clock by now. They left the spoils of their dinner, crumpled napkins, melted ice-cream, flies drowning in half-empty glasses, for the bar down below. The whiskey came out straight away, for you had to give the young couple a good send-off, make it a day to remember. They'd all been waiting for this, for the seri-ous drinking to begin.

Brendan and Eileen led off the dancing, grinning, and soon others got up on the floor. The band played, and the young girls mooned and swayed, while the fellows looked and joked, couples clung, and old men boozed. Noreen sipped a vodka and watched, remembering her own time, living and dancing in a dream, before she became aware of the sordidness beneath. How it all caught you, like a frenzy, a mania . . .

'Would you like to dance?'

She sighed. She just wanted to be left alone, to reflect, to sum up; to capture everything. She turned, and to her surprise it was Eileen's brother, Michael, standing there. It was strange to see him smart in dark suit and tie, stiff collar. He was a bit red-faced, whether from embarrass-ment or drink, she couldn't tell.

He smelled of beer, as Kenny had once – the beginning of it all. Michael held her carefully, a little distance from him, not too close.

'It went well, then,' she commented.

'Aye, it did, aye,' he agreed.

'It'll be you next, I suppose.' She didn't know why she said that. She always hated it when people said it to her. Just something to say.

He was grinning in an odd, embarrassed sort of way. 'Ach, not at all. Not for a while yet, anyhow. Sure there's other things to be done first.'

He was silent then, looking away across her shoulder, and she could scrutinize his face in safety. He'd lost the sullen, adolescent look, which she knew so well. How old was he, anyway? Twenty, maybe, a couple of years older than Eileen and her. She could see him in the Army somehow, maybe because of his height and his brown hair which had been all cropped for the wedding. There were wee freckles over his nose, which had a Roman hump on it.

He looked down at her suddenly, and she looked away.

'Still going off to study, then?'

She nodded.

'Ah, it's well for some,' he said, 'to have brains . . . I'm going across the water too, you know,' he added then, with a touch of pride.

'Oh? Whatever for?' It seemed so unlikely, somehow. Surely he wasn't the sort to leave.

'I have a job with an engineering firm over there,' he said. 'A big one. Two years' training on full pay – free flights home and all.'

'What about your Ma, then?'

'What about yours?'

She smiled.

He would be in Birmingham, he said. 'I could come down and see you some time . . .' He looked at her questioningly. His eyes were grey-green, more muted than Eileen's.

'All right, then.' She nodded. 'I'd like that.'

He gave her arm a squeeze. 'Come on, I'll buy you a drink.'

They stood at the bar together, watching the dancing. Mr McAllister pointed at them from across the room and waved. Michael shook his head slowly, and laughed. 'Ach, he's full,' he said. 'The ould man's full.'

'Well, hasn't he a right to be,' said Noreen, 'on his daughter's wedding day?'

They could see Eileen, still in her white, twirling in and out of everyone, then caught by her father, both of them proud of each other, on this day.

'She's lovely, isn't she?' said Noreen, still watching them.

'Aye, I suppose so,' said Michael. He sounded surprised, as if he had never considered the possibility before. He lit up a cigarette, offered her one.

Noreen blew out the smoke, and it soothed her. 'Ach, God,' she said. 'We're all moving on, aren't we? I mean things are never the same again, it's all over.'

He looked at her, perplexed. 'Aye,' he agreed, doubtfully.

'Her,' Noreen nodded her head in Eileen's direction. 'She's married. And me – I'm leaving . . .'

Mrs McAllister in her pink was dancing with some ould fellow, beaming away. He was a bit fragile-looking beside her ample figure, white-haired, but he'd a rare smile on his face. Mrs McAllister was blowing a bit, but she was surprisingly nimble for someone so large.

'Sure what is there here?' said Michael, pursuing the lapsed conversation. 'Sure what is there?' He was staring into his glass, a bit morose. Noreen knocked back her own drink, shivered. She felt a bit cold, all of a sudden.

This dance was coming to an end. Noreen could feel it. Old men, drunk with alcohol and too much youth, were slumped in chairs; young couples stood close in corners; just a few middle-aged ones swept the floor, remembering. There was no sign of Eileen. Brendan was talking to Mr and Mrs McAllister, his parents-in-law, on the comfy seats. A few people were looking at their watches. The band wooed sleep.

Then Eileen appeared in the doorway. She had discarded her white and wore instead a cream suit with navy squiggles on it. She had a navy hat, matching shoes, and even navy elbow-length gloves. Oh, and a navy bag.

The band suddenly sprang back to life with an old jazz tune, and the whole wedding was re-created in that instant. In fact, this was the wedding; for Noreen, at least. It wasn't the ceremony, nor the reception: those weren't what it was all about. This was it: the leave-taking. And she'd only just realized. The moment was so nostalgic (yet how many times had it happened before, only to different people?), and Eileen looked so beautiful, as if she'd stepped right out of an old film, that Noreen wanted to cry. She was taken by surprise.

Everyone else had woken up and was staring at the vision in the doorway. Eileen walked into the room, and everyone stared, but dared not go near her, lest they break the moment. She was lovely, and Noreen could feel the tears coming, although till now the wedding had not moved her. She had not expected it to. After all, Eileen would still be here, as before; it was Noreen who was doing the leaving. Eileen would be the same, surely? – only married. That was what she had thought.

But now Eileen stood before her in the elegant, cream and navy suit, and they found themselves staring at each other's tears. Eileen was leaving. This was how it had always been: the girl leaving her mother's house and going to a new one, her husband's. Mrs McAllister was crying, as mothers always had. They could hear her – muffled animal sounds in her handkerchief. So raw.

'Don't go!'

Eileen smiled, wiping her eyes. 'What d'you mean, don't go?'

She sniffed, and sat down beside Noreen. 'I suppose we might have known,' she said, 'that it would end up like this. You – going away to study. You were always like that, really, Noreen.'

'And you married . . .'

Eileen looked down at the ring. 'Aye. D'you remember,' she said, 'those Sunday afternoons, when we used to walk the roads? Looking for talent?' She laughed. 'And we used to plan how we'd get married and live near each other.'

Noreen nodded. 'And we'd wheel the babies out together, sit in the park. How grand it would all have been . . .'

'You're making my mascara run.' Eileen dabbed carefully at her eyes with a white lacy hanky. 'Here – you'll come back a professor or something, ever so la di da, much too good for the likes of us!'

'No – I'll be just the same. And I'll be coming back to visit, you know.'

'Anyhow, it's well for you, getting out of this hole. I'd go, if I could.'

But they both knew it wasn't true. Eileen wouldn't ever go. This was her place, somehow, in a way that it could never now be Noreen's. Even so, Noreen didn't want to be the one to leave. Oh, it tore at her to have to leave this hole, this dump, which other people could complain about, because they didn't have to go.

'I don't want to,' she said to Eileen. 'I don't want to be the one to leave.'

'But you always were leaving,' said Eileen. 'Somehow, you always were . . .' She hesitated and touched Noreen's bent head.

Noreen looked up at her. 'D'you know, Eileen, if it weren't for you – I mean, if we didn't know one another, then my children would grow up hating yours, and yours mine, all because they wouldn't know each other; they would never have the chance to find out that the others were only children, just like them, just the same; they would see only little monsters . . .'

Eileen was holding her hand. The band was playing the twist. There were whoops and laughter from the couples on the floor.

'But we do know each other, Noreen, we do. Look – you just have to carry on, you just have to go on with things – don't let it stop you, the hatred, the fear. That's a way of fighting. Only carry on, somehow, you have to live . . .'

Brendan was there behind them, waiting.

'I have to go now, they're all waiting. I have to go.' She sat there still, another minute. Then Eileen hugged her friend, Noreen, and they clung together, not caring about the people watching. It would be the only time.

Then Eileen was walking to the door with Brendan, and Noreen couldn't get through for the crowd that surged after them, all wanting to see them off. This was what they had been waiting for; a bit of fun. They stood about in the cold night air, yawning, trying to shake off sloth, throwing half-hearted confetti, and Noreen couldn't get through.

The car doors slammed, and she could hear the tin cans rattle. People laughed. She knew that all across the back was scrawled JUST MARRIED, so that everyone would know. There were cries of 'Good luck!', and the men shouted, 'Get on in there, boy!' The revving of the engine filled the night with exhaust fumes. Noreen tried in vain to see over the bobbing heads.

Then Brendan let in the clutch and the car, some old banger, roared off amidst cheers; it paused at the top of the drive, then was off, clattering down the road. The lights soon disappeared.

Now only the guests were left. They began yawning again, collected coats, and made for their cars, the job done. Noreen still stood in her flimsy dress, staring down the road and biting her lip; but the tears trickled down her cheeks anyway. People brushed past her, jolting, and someone caught the back of her dress, tearing it. It didn't matter now, though.

Noreen turned round, and there was Mrs McAllister, a large woman who read the tea leaves and cleaned in the hospital; her red hands plucked at tears, and she was all dressed in silly pink. But Mrs McAllister didn't care. She didn't care if people saw her cry; she was only doing what women had always done. Her daughter had gone. She cried, and could think of nothing else.

She saw Noreen, the wee Protestant girl, standing there alone. They wept in each other's arms, Noreen and Mrs McAllister: the left behind.

FOR THE BEST IN PAPERBACKS, LOOK FOR THE

In every corner of the world, on every subject under the sun, Penguin represents quality and variety – the very best in publishing today.

For complete information about books available from Penguin – including Pelicans, Puffins, Peregrines and Penguin Classics – and how to order them, write to us at the appropriate address below. Please note that for copyright reasons the selection of books varies from country to country.

In the United Kingdom: Please write to *Dept E.P., Penguin Books Ltd, Harmondsworth, Middlesex, UB7 0DA*

If you have any difficulty in obtaining a title, please send your order with the correct money, plus ten per cent for postage and packaging, to *PO Box No 11, West Drayton, Middlesex*

In the United States: Please write to *Dept BA, Penguin, 299 Murray Hill Parkway, East Rutherford, New Jersey 07073*

In Canada: Please write to *Penguin Books Canada Ltd, 2801 John Street, Markham, Ontario L3R 1B4*

In Australia: Please write to the *Marketing Department, Penguin Books Australia Ltd, P.O. Box 257, Ringwood, Victoria 3134*

In New Zealand: Please write to the *Marketing Department, Penguin Books (NZ) Ltd, Private Bag, Takapuna, Auckland 9*

In India: Please write to *Penguin Overseas Ltd, 706 Eros Apartments, 56 Nehru Place, New Delhi, 110019*

In Holland: Please write to *Penguin Books Nederland B.V., Postbus 195, NL–1380AD Weesp, Netherlands*

In Germany: Please write to *Penguin Books Ltd, Friedrichstrasse 10–12, D–6000 Frankfurt Main 1, Federal Republic of Germany*

In Spain: Please write to *Longman Penguin España, Calle San Nicolas 15, E–28013 Madrid, Spain*

In France: Please write to *Penguin Books Ltd, 39 Rue de Montmorency, F-75003, Paris, France*

In Japan: Please write to *Longman Penguin Japan Co Ltd, Yamaguchi Building, 2-12-9 Kanda Jimbocho, Chiyoda-Ku, Tokyo 101, Japan*